THE COVENANT BOOK ONE - THE FALL

BY
A.J.M

"God blesses those who patiently endure testing and temptation. Afterward, they will receive the crown of life that God has promised to those who love him."
James 1:12 NLT

Prologue - Story of the First Saints
7

Chapter 1 - Malachi Shaka
12

Chapter 2- One Day
25

Chapter 3- Return If Possible
35

Chapter 4-Tribute
48

Chapter 5-Founding Father
62

Chapter 6- New Era
72

Chapter 7- Gang
83

Chapter 8- People Person
98

chapter 9-Royalties
111

Chapter 10- Soiree Incident
130

Chapter 11- Soiree Incident PT.2
143

Chapter 12- Soiree Incident PT.3
163

Chapter 13 - Soiree Incident Pt.4
176

Chapter 14 - Soiree Incident Pt.5
189

Chapter 15- Soiree Incident Pt.6
200

Chapter 16- Soiree Incident Pt.7
211

Chapter 17- Soiree Incident Pt.8
224

Chapter 18- Soirée Incident PT.9
238

Chapter 19- Soirée Incident PT.10
247

Chapter 20- Soiree Incident Final. PT
265

Chapter 21- tranquil
280

Chapter 22- The Calvary
295

Chapter 22- Not Just Luck
306

Chapter 23- M.O.G
318

Chapter 24- Secrets
332

Chapter 25- Dark Clouds
342

Chapter 26- Slow down
359

Chapter 26- The Night
373

Chapter 27- Reflection
382

Chapter 28- Y Murder
394

Chapter 29- Where There Is Smoke there is fire
407

Chapter 30- Talk the Truth
419

Chapter 31- Figure it out
431

Chapter 32- Te Amo
443

Chapter 33- Cree
457

PROLOGUE - STORY OF THE FIRST SAINTS

In the Age of Creation, when the world was birthed from the symphony of the divine, angels of pure light soared through the heavens, servants of the Almighty's vision. Humanity, woven from flesh and spirit, emerged as beacons of divine love, destined to be the Almighty's loyal stewards.

Yet, within this celestial harmony, a dark seed took root. Dragon, an angel consumed by ambition and greed, looked upon the Almighty's power with envy. He sought to reshape the world in his own twisted image, rallying a legion of fallen angels to his cause.

The resulting rebellion shook the very foundations of the cosmos, as Dragon's army of silver-tongued rebels stormed the gates of heaven. In a cataclysmic tempest, the Almighty, in righteous fury, cast Dragon and his followers down to the mortal realm, their celestial light dimmed, their bodies bound by the earth's embrace.

Though imprisoned, Dragon's ambition only burned brighter. He whispered seductive promises of forbidden power into the hearts of humanity, twisting and corrupting souls, driving a wedge between kin and community. A dystopian shadow fell over the world, as the fallen angels enslaved humanity under their oppressive rule.

Observing his creation in torment, the Almighty devised a grand strategy - Spiritual Energy, the very essence of one's soul, a potent force that could empower humans to confront the fallen. Yet, this energy was a double-edged sword, susceptible to corruption and capable of amplifying evil.

To champion the liberation of humanity, the Almighty chose four men, their souls unyielding, their hearts pure, bestowing upon them the power of the Saints - an unprecedented mastery of Spiritual Energy and their inherent abilities.

Shaka, the Lunar Oracle, harnessed lunar aspects to sway the bounds of reality. Jones, the Melody Sculptor, manipulated sound waves with surgical precision. Edwards, the Elemental Strategist, commanded the spectrum of temperatures. And Johnson, the Seismic Sentinel, wielded vigilance and sheer will, crushing foes with earth-rending shockwaves.

These legendary abilities etched deep within their souls were but the beginning. Spiritual Energy empowered them to transcend the limits of mortality, harnessing a wellspring of strength that soared with each battle.

The Saints led a new generation of warriors into the light of Spiritual Awakening - a profound realization of their true nature. Awakenings, evoked by near-death experiences or moments of unparalleled clarity, unlocked unique abilities in each warrior, revealing their soul's potential.

As champions of hope, the Awakened spearheaded the charge against the fallen angels. Emboldened by the Saints' leadership and Spiritual Energy, humanity rose in defiance, meeting the crimson dawn with unwavering courage.

A cataclysmic holy war erupted, reshaping mountains and rending the skies. Days of relentless battle unfolded, paled in the resonant light of divine and demonic clashes. At last, the humans triumphed, forcing the fallen back into the abyss.

The Almighty, witnessing the victory, forged Hell - a dimension of pure darkness - a prison to contain Dragon and his legion, forever severed from the world they sought to dominate.

The Saints established their empire in the heart of the Caribbean, a bastion against lingering shadows, where clans of awakened warriors guarded humanity against darkness's looming whispers - a legacy enduring across generations, their true nature shrouded in myth and legend.

Though the darkness sleeps, the echoes of ambition still murmur in the shadows, poised for the day balance shifts again. The world remains vigilant against the crimson dawn that could rise anew, a testament to the Saints' unwavering courage and eternal watch.

CHAPTER 1 - MALACHI SHAKA

The steam from the shower billowed, obscuring the white tiles of the opulent bathroom in a shroud of mist. Malachi let the scalding water cascade over his body, hoping it could wash away the grief that threatened to consume him.

Tears mingled with the streams of water tracing down his face, leaving salty tracks on his skin. He leaned against the cool, smooth wall, his damp white locs clinging to his head as he struggled to keep himself upright.

Malachi's amber eyes, the signature eyes of the Shaka clan, stared blankly at the swirling water disappearing down the drain. They reflected the turmoil raging within him—the gaping wound left by his father's absence, a constant ache that gnawed at his soul.

Through the mist, a towering figure emerged—a phantom in a crisp purple suit, long flowing dreads reaching out to him in a silent plea. The scent of old leather and peppermint filled the air, a ghostly echo of his father's presence.

Malachi choked back a sob, his body trembling under the weight of his grief. In this opulent sanctuary adorned with Shaka symbols, he felt utterly alone, adrift in an ocean of sorrow. The luxurious trappings offered no comfort; the only solace he craved was the embrace of the father he had lost.

His father had been a legendary captain, known for his unwavering courage and strategic brilliance—a legacy Malachi felt the weight of every day.

A minute later, he faced the mirror, his reflection sharp and clear. Dressed in a pristine white suit, the fabric smooth against his skin, a black undershirt peeked from the collar. He raised his hand, thumb tracing the obsidian band on his finger, a white crescent moon etched into its surface.

The ring felt heavy, a constant reminder of the legacy he carried and the responsibility that weighed heavily on his shoulders.

His phone buzzed on the dresser, the sharp chime cutting through the quiet.

Over a hundred messages flooded in, all offering condolences.

He sighed deeply, brushing his locs out of his face before tapping on Miguel's message: "*Yo, you ready? We're about to head out. Are you rolling with us, or doing your own thing?"*

Malachi pondered. *Don't wanna travel with so many people,* he thought. Just then, a soft knock on the door was followed by an angelic voice. "Mal, you in there?"

He looked up, relief washing over him. "Thank God," he muttered under his breath.

"Coming!" he called back, quickly typing a reply to Miguel: "*Coming on my own."*

Pocketing his phone, he opened the door.

Standing there was a vision: Bianca. Her vibrant pink dreads were styled in a sleek ponytail, cascading down her back like a waterfall of fire. Playful curls framed her face, accentuating her striking features, while a series of piercings adorned her nose.

She wore a one-shoulder black dress with a daring slit, revealing just enough to intrigue. An ornate necklace crafted with the intricate Shaka crescent moon symbol completed her look, making her seem like a goddess descended from the heavens.

She was his best friend, always there for him, a source of unwavering support and understanding.

"Hi," she said, her voice sweet and soothing, like a melody that calmed the storm within him.

Malachi took a deep breath, his heart racing. "Oh, you came," he said, his voice a little unsteady, betraying the turmoil inside him.

Bianca stepped closer and wrapped her arms around him, pulling him into a warm embrace. "I'm so sorry this happened," she whispered, her voice soft and sincere. "I'm sorry I didn't text or call—graduation was just so hectic. But I'm here now."

Malachi felt the weight of her words, the genuine concern in her tone easing some of his sorrow. He held onto her, grateful for her presence.

He invited her in, and as she stepped inside, her gaze swept across the room. The space was modern and sleek, with a blend of muted tones and vibrant accents. A plush bed lay at the center, its covers slightly rumpled, while a gaming setup with a glowing monitor occupied one corner. Neon lights cast a soft glow, reflecting off the polished floor, and a cozy chair sat invitingly nearby.

Bianca settled at the edge of the bed, her posture poised yet relaxed, clutching her purse in her lap. Malachi joined her, the mattress shifting slightly under their combined weight. He could feel the warmth emanating from her as she looked at him with genuine concern.

"How are you doing?" she asked gently.

"I'm alright," he replied, trying to sound more composed than he felt.

She placed a comforting hand on his shoulder, her touch grounding him. "Are you alright?"

He smiled, a bit uncertain. "Yeah, yeah, I am."

She tilted her head, a knowing look in her eyes. "Mhmm," she said, sensing the layers beneath his words. He wondered if she truly understood the depth of his feelings.

Then, shifting her focus, she asked, "How's your brother holding up?" Malachi paused, a flicker of irritation passing through his eyes.

"Well, Miguel is being Miguel—always cracking jokes," Bianca replied. "That's just his way of dealing with it."

She touched him lightly, a casual gesture that felt warm and reassuring. "But on the bright side," she said, holding his hand, "I finished college and I'm back now. I'm not going anywhere."

"I'll be here for both of you."

He offered her a small smile, the tension easing slightly. "Thanks, B. That means a lot."

The sound of multiple car engines roared to life outside, vibrations reverberating through the walls.

She glanced at him, a question in her eyes. "You ready?"

Malachi gazed up at the ceiling, his thoughts a tangled web.

"No," he admitted, his voice barely a whisper.

"Not really."

Bianca chuckled softly, standing up and extending her hand. "Come on, I got you."

He took her hand, allowing her strength to pull him up.

They walked outside, stepping into the sprawling grounds of the mansion. The estate was a testament to the Shaka's wealth and power. The gardens were filled with ancient trees and exotic flowers, each carefully chosen to represent the strength and resilience of the Shaka lineage. Even the air seemed to hold a sense of history and power.

Cars were lined up, some already pulling out onto the long driveway. The sky was a somber black, fitting for the occasion.

As they made their way toward a sleek black BMW, a voice called out, "Yo!"

Malachi turned to see a young man standing on the mansion's steps, looking barely older than a teenager. He fumbled with his green jacket, trying to put it on while a toothbrush hung loosely from his mouth. His large dreads, adorned with beads at the tips, bounced as he left his belt unbuckled.

Deon was Malachi's cousin, the son of his uncle, a man known for his ruthless ambition and cunning. Malachi had always been rude to Deon, their rivalry rooted in a childhood marked by sharp insults and a constant struggle for attention.

The young man held out a folded paper to Malachi, a hint of disdain in his eyes.

With his hands still in his pockets, Malachi smirked and asked, "What's this?"

The young man stepped closer, shoving the paper against Malachi's chest with little regard. "My dad wants you to do the eulogy."

Malachi frowned, bewilderment flickering across his face. "Isn't he supposed to be the one doing it?"

"Well, he said he's gonna be late, so you gotta do it," Deon shot back, his tone dripping with annoyance.

Malachi thought, *Late to your own brother's funeral? That's kinda crazy.*

"Does Gramps know about this?" he questioned, raising an eyebrow in disbelief.

The young man sighed, exasperated. "Yo, just take the damn paper."

Malachi snatched the paper, barely hiding his irritation, as Deon called out,

"Hey, Bianca," spotting her on the other side of the car, clearly eager to escape the tension.

She smiled and waved.

With that, Deon turned and went back inside.

Malachi slipped into the passenger seat of the BMW, Bianca taking her place behind the wheel.

She started the car and glanced over at him. "What was all that?"

"Your guess is as good as mine," Malachi said, staring out the window.

As they drove off, the weight of the day settled over them.

The somber drive to the cemetery was filled with silence. Bianca's presence was a steady comfort, her gaze often drifting over to him, a silent assurance of support.

The weight of his grief, the shock of his father's sudden passing, the impending responsibility of the eulogy, and the looming presence of the Shaka legacy all settled upon him like a heavy cloak.

As they approached the cemetery, the sound of mourners' hushed voices filtered through the open windows.

As they pulled into the clearing deep within the woods, the sight of the assembled crowd, the white banners adorned with the Shaka crest, and the ethereal glow of the moon overhead felt surreal—a dream he couldn't wake up from.

Bianca parked the car a short distance away, a silent understanding hanging between them.

Malachi took a deep breath, the familiar scent of damp earth and moss hitting his nostrils, the aroma of his family's history intertwined with nature.

The crowd dressed entirely in white, moved with a quiet reverence among the towering ancient trees.

To Be Continued...

CHAPTER 2- ONE DAY

Bianca stepped out of the car, the moss-covered ground squishing softly beneath her heels.

The cool, damp night air carried the scent of river water and pine needles, while the rhythmic beat of traditional drums echoed from the riverside, drawing her in.

She glanced at Malachi beside her, his expression grim, a crumpled piece of paper trembling in his hand.

"Hold up, let me see what it says," he muttered, his voice a rough rasp as he scanned the message, anger twisting his features.

"What is it? What's wrong?" Bianca stepped closer, urgency lacing her tone.

Malachi's eyes narrowed, his jaw tightening. He crushed the paper in his fist, exhaling sharply.

"You've gotta be kidding me," he snapped, disbelief heavy in his voice.

His arms were on the roof of the car, his gaze fixed on the night. "They want me to spread some nonsense," Malachi spat.

"He's always trying to mess things up with my dad."

Bianca's heart sank at the mention of Peter.

"What did he do?" she asked, glancing at the solemn faces gathered by the riverside, listening intently to the ceremony.

As Malachi read the eulogy, his voice faltered.

"Today, we remember my father, 'The King of Empty Promises.' He had a knack for grand plans but never followed through.

Despite everything, I learned resilience from him. Rest in peace, Dad."

Bianca's face dropped. "Are you serious? Ugh." Malachi looked around the garden, feeling the weight of her disappointment.

"No, Mal, this is horrible. Why would he even do that to his brother?" Bianca breathed, outrage shaking her voice.

"Probably to disgrace my father so he can take over as the head of the family," Malachi said, tossing the crumpled paper far into the dark. It struck a nearby tree with a loud crack, chipping off a small piece of bark.

"He put me in the hospital before, so I'm not surprised. Peter's always been obsessed with power.

He knows that if he can undermine Dad's reputation, he can position himself as the better choice for the clan head. It's all about control for him."

Bianca shook her head firmly. "That will never happen, Mal. Peter's arrogance will be his downfall. He might think he can manipulate us, but he'll get what's coming to him. You're not alone in this. We'll make sure everyone sees the truth."

A slow smile broke across Malachi's face. "What would I do without you, B?" he asked, gratitude mingling with relief.

"You'd probably be in jail," she quipped, her playful tone offering a brief respite from the weight of their situation.

As they approached the assembly, the rhythmic beat of drums and flutes intensified, drawing them closer to the heart of the ceremony, where their family's legacy awaited.

Rows of white-draped chairs hugged the riverbank beneath the moon's silver glow, a pristine white carpet tracing a solemn path to the center where a white tent stood, its fabric billowing gently in the night breeze.

Members from the Hearts, Shakas, Johnsons, Edwards, and Jones clans filled the chairs, their faces softly illuminated by lanterns swinging from moss-draped branches, casting flickering shadows across their determined expressions.

The air buzzed with anticipation, and soft sniffles echoed, tears streaming down some faces.

These were not just ordinary members; many knew the hidden truths that bound them all.

Teenage girls in flowing white gowns danced gracefully, their movements echoing resilience and unity.

The white carpet glowed underfoot, reflecting lantern light and moonbeams alike, while the haunting music wove through the trees, creating a living tapestry of sound and motion.

The duo wove through the assembly, friendly faces greeted them with nods and murmurs.

Malachi responded warmly, but amidst the laughter, he heard soft sobbing.

A striking woman rose, tears glistening on her polished mahogany skin.

Her short platinum hair framed her features, and the floral-patterned blue dress flowed gracefully around her.

Malachi approached her, and she embraced him tightly, transferring silent strength.

Continuing to the front row, Malachi locked eyes with his brother, Miguel.

A genuine smile lit Miguel's face as he extended his hand.

They shared a heartfelt embrace, lingering in the moment.

"Heck took you so long," Miguel murmured, his voice laden with emotion. Their hands tapped twice, index fingers locking in a brief, meaningful grip before breaking away, the gesture rich with unspoken camaraderie.

He turned to Bianca, his smile warm. "Hey, B," he greeted, gently touching her arm.

"Hey, Miguel," she replied softly, squeezing his hand reassuringly. "You holding up okay? Just know I'm here for you."

Miguel nodded gratitude in his smile. "Thanks, B. It means a lot."

"We're in this together," Bianca added sincerely.

"We'll get through it, I promise."

As they took their seats, a sense of collective strength enveloped them, the community's support palpable as they awaited the next part of the ceremony.

Six of Malachi's uncles entered, carrying a polished casket.

The sight was arresting, the black surface gleaming under the lantern light. Intricately carved into it was a full moon, its round form radiating mystery, while the initials E.I.S. nestled within the detailed lunar patterns, adding an enigmatic touch to the already captivating design.

Malachi froze, breath catching in his throat.

Beside the casket was a picture of his father, smiling warmly in a sunlit garden.

The dancing ceased, and a profound silence filled the area.

Each uncle passed Malachi, exchanging firm daps.

The last uncle patted his shoulder, whispering, "It's gonna be alright, you hear me?" Malachi nodded, heart heavy yet resolute.

A dark-skinned girl with crescent moon-shaped earrings walked to the center of the white tent, dressed in a chic white halter-neck jumpsuit.

Her presence signaled the next part of the ceremony, anticipation filling the air.

The dark-skinned girl with intricately braided hair and crescent moon-shaped earrings stepped forward, commanding the attention of the gathered crowd.

"Good evening, everyone," she said solemnly.

A wave of hushed whispers rippled through the assembly as Miguel leaned in and whispered to Malachi, "When did Catherine get back?"

Malachi shrugged, equally surprised.

Catherine then spoke up, her voice carrying a sorrowful lilt.

"I wish this gathering was under better circumstances.

But I am grateful to be here with all of you, to honor the memory of a great man."

She turned and motioned to Malachi. "And now, we will hear the eulogy from Malachi."

Miguel's eyes widened as he turned to his brother.

"When did this happen?" he asked in a hushed tone, his surprise palpable.

Malachi placed a reassuring hand on Miguel's arm, a flicker of surprise quickly replaced by composure.

"Today," he murmured, a hint of rueful amusement coloring his tone.

Miguel's eyes widened in disbelief, his mouth opening and closing as if grappling for words.

He turned to Bianca, his face a portrait of astonishment.

Bianca shrugged in response, her expression one of resigned acceptance.

With a deep breath, Malachi rose from his seat and went to the center of the tent.

As he approached the microphone, he felt the eyes of the gathered clansmen upon him, their expressions a mix of sorrow, expectation, and unwavering support.

Malachi paused, letting the rhythm of the drums and the gentle whisper of the river provide a somber backdrop.

Then, with a steady voice, he began to speak.

> To be continued...

CHAPTER 3- RETURN IF POSSIBLE

The weight of the moment pressed down on Malachi, a suffocating blanket of grief.

He flicked his thumb against his nose, a nervous gesture that did little to soothe the turmoil within.

The air thrummed with a collective sorrow, heavy and palpable.

Drawing a deep breath, he raised his voice, tinged with solemnity.

"First off, I wanna say, God is good."

A murmur rippled through the crowd gathered under the white tent, a collective acknowledgment in the somber air.

The scent of lilies and damp earth hung heavy, a stark reminder of the finality of the occasion.

"So, how's everyone doing tonight?"

His eyes scanned the faces before him, finally settling on Miguel and Bianca.

 Bianca gave him an encouraging nod, and he managed a faint smile, his heart heavy.

"I know everyone has an expectation of what I'm supposed to say," he began, his voice trembling slightly.

"Some want me to say my dad was crazy, that he killed himself. But that's far from the truth."

He gazed down at the polished casket, his vision blurring with tears.

The polished surface was too much to bear, its gleaming perfection a stark contrast to the raw grief that swelled within him. He knew his father would have hated the polished wood, its smooth surface a breeding ground for germs, a thought that sent a shiver down his spine.

"He saw his family as a reflection of himself.

He always did what he thought was best for us – not just for us, but for the whole island.

I learned a lot from him, and I know how I want to live the rest of my life because of him.

I wish 'RIP' meant 'return if possible,' but I know that's not possible."

He looked up again, swallowing hard as the grief clawed at his throat. The tears welled in his eyes, threatening to spill over, but he held them back, a familiar, almost involuntary reaction to the raw emotions swirling around him.

"Put up your lighters for him," he urged, his voice breaking.

One by one, lighters flicked open, tiny flames illuminating the mourning faces of the crowd.

The heat of the flames momentarily chased away the damp chill of the air, offering a flicker of warmth in the cold abyss of their loss.

Malachi looked over at Catherine, who pressed her lips together in empathy and patted his back gently.

He felt her touch, but a fleeting shiver of discomfort ran through him.

He knew he should be grateful for her support, but the touch of another's hand always left him feeling slightly uneasy.

With a resolute breath, he walked to the casket, his heart aching.

He paused, hesitated for a moment, his hand hovering just inches above the polished surface.

Finally, he reached out, his fingertips barely grazing the wood, a hesitant touch that spoke volumes of his internal struggle.

"Even though you're gone, your memory still lives on," he whispered, his eyes welling up with tears.

"Travel safe," he added, his voice choked with emotion.

He kissed his fingers, a gesture he had learned from his father, and tenderly touched the symbol engraved on the casket, a final farewell to the man who had shaped his life in ways words could scarcely capture.

The symbol was intricate, carved into the wood with precision.

" Sleep in peace, Dad."

The flames of the lighters flickered in the dim light of dusk, a poignant tribute to a life that had burned brightly, now extinguished but never forgotten.

Malachi stepped away from the casket, turning to see Miguel and Bianca approaching.

His heart ached at the sight of Miguel's red, tear-filled eyes.

The sight of his brother's raw emotion stirred a deep empathy within him.

He knew Miguel was struggling to hold back his grief, just as he was.

"Come here, man," Malachi said, opening his arms wide.

Miguel rushed to him. Malachi held the back of Miguel's head, their foreheads touching, as Miguel broke down in his embrace. They shared the weight of their loss in silent support.

"I know, bro.

I know," he whispered, his voice laden with the weight of their shared grief.

His eyes caught sight of Bianca, her lone figure standing against the backdrop of the twilight.

Tears streamed down her cheeks as she gazed sorrowfully at the sky, a silent plea to the Most High.

He knew she was grieving too, her pain etched on her face, a silent echo of his own.

Malachi extended his hand toward her, his own emotions threatening to boil over.

Meeting his gaze, Bianca crossed the distance.

She moved with a grace that reminded him of a wilting flower, fragile yet strong.

Without a word, she stepped into the circle of his arms, and Malachi held them both tightly.

His head dropped a gesture of humility and unity amid the anguish.

Catherine watched them from the side, her composure barely holding.

The pain etched lines on her face, and she blinked back tears as she continued her speech.

"We gather here to honor a man whose spirit touched every one of us," Catherine's voice faltered but regained its strength.

 "We remember not his end, but the life he lived and the legacy he left us."

As Catherine continued, Malachi walked Miguel and Bianca back to their seats.

They sat down, the exhaustion of their emotions weighing heavily upon them.

Suddenly, a firm hand rested on Malachi's shoulder, jolting him back to the present.

His Uncle Aron stood there, his eyes filled with a grave yet determined look.

The touch of Aron's hand on his shoulder sent a jolt of discomfort through him.

He slowly looked down at the hand, its calloused skin a stark contrast to the smooth, polished surface he preferred.

He recoiled slightly, a fleeting gesture that went unnoticed by his uncle.

"Malachi," Aron began in a low voice, "we need to talk later.

And Gramps said he wants you both to come by the mansion tomorrow," Aron added, his voice carrying the weight of something significant.

Malachi nodded, his heart racing and thoughts scattered.

He glanced at Miguel, who wiped his tear-streaked face and gave a faint nod of understanding.

They both knew that their ancestral home held deeper layers of family secrets and duties they were yet to uncover.

Catherine's voice interrupted their thoughts.

"We will now follow the Shaka family traditions, led by the eldest uncle, Aron."

Aron patted Malachi's back before stepping toward the casket.

 He winked at Catherine, drawing a bittersweet smile from her teary eyes.

As Aron reached the casket, his eyes took on a shimmering blue hue.

The atmosphere grew dense and heavy as if an invisible weight was pressing down on everything around him.

Malachi's skin tingled, and a shiver raced down his spine, leaving him breathless in the face of such an overwhelming presence.

He could almost feel the earth itself pulsating beneath his feet.

Aron's voice, low and steady, filled the small space. "Enoch lived and died a true Shaka," he said, the word hanging in the air like a promise.

"More than a brother, he was the father I never knew I needed.

Shaka men don't surrender, not in life, not in death. His path was our father's path, our ancestors' path...and it's mine."

He paused, his gaze distant, seemingly lost in the memory of his brother.
A flicker of cold fire ignited in his eyes. "Some debts," he murmured, almost to himself, "are settled only in blood. The earth will remember Enoch. And so will I."

Aron, his jacket slung over his shoulders, reached out. His bare arm, pale against the dark wood, touched the casket.

Moonstone, a liquid light, flowed from his fingertips, instantly encasing the coffin in a shimmering, moon-rock shell.

 It solidified around it like ice freezing around a fallen leaf.

A collective gasp rippled through the seated mourners; hushed whispers, choked sobs, and awed silence mixed in the air.

Slowly, Aron raised his hand; the moon-rock casket, seemingly weightless, began to sink into the earth.

He clenched his fist, and with a sharp, almost silent *shhhht*, a tombstone, polished like obsidian, spurted from the ground, the Shaka family symbol blazing in ethereal light upon its surface.

The Shaka family symbol appeared on the tombstone, etched with precision.

Malachi's eyes narrowed, his gaze hardening as it fixed upon the glowing words, "RIP Enoch Shaka."

His lips pressed into a thin line, a subtle clench in his jaw revealing the tension simmering beneath his calm exterior.

The glow was almost taunting, a reminder of the legacy he was all too aware of yet wished he could ignore.

As the light danced across his face, the flicker in his eyes betrayed a deep-seated distaste, the kind that twisted his insides and stiffened his shoulders.

He sat silent, the air around him heavy with unspoken animosity.

To be continued...

CHAPTER 4- TRIBUTE

The garden whispered with the rustle of leaves as Malachi deftly navigated the gaps in the somber crowd, his hands buried deep in his pockets to contain the turmoil within.

Bianca, gliding beside him, broke the silence with a gentle, "Dre called. He wanted to be here, but he's still stuck in the UK."

"I know," Malachi replied, the words laced with unspoken sorrow, his eyes reflecting loss that words couldn't convey.

Miguel trailed behind, his usual buoyancy replaced by raw vulnerability.

"Dad could've made us laugh even now," he murmured, his voice trembling before crumbling beneath the weight of his emotions.

The grief flooded over him, his jovial facade giving way to a torrent of longing.

Bianca wrapped him in a comforting embrace, her presence a steady anchor amid the storm of his tears. Malachi stood close, his eyes heavy with empathy, yearning to bridge the gap between his reticence and his brother's open grief.

Amidst the trees and the soft light of the moon, the trio remained, bound in shared sorrow and the silent promise of their father's enduring presence in every tear, every sigh, and every stolen glance.

From the shadows, a man in an immaculate white security uniform approached. His presence was a serene blend of authority and respect.

Pausing before Malachi, he nodded gently. "Your mother is here and wishes to see you," he said, his voice a respectful murmur against the night.

Miguel's eyes went wide. "Wait, she's here?" he exclaimed, his voice alive with shock and excitement. He took a step back, exchanging a glance with Bianca as they briefly parted, each absorbing the surprise.

The security officer nodded. "Yes, she just flew in.

She's at your father's tombstone."

Without another word, Miguel took off running, his footsteps echoing in the night.

Malachi paused, looking at the security officer. "Appreciate it, man," he said, his voice steady.

The officer, maintaining professional poise, nodded.

The security officer's gaze fell, his voice heavy with remorse. "I'm truly sorry we couldn't do more to save your father," he said quietly, the weight of his words hanging in the air.

Malachi patted the security officer's shoulder. "It's all good," he said with a reassuring nod, dismissing the weight of the moment.

"You couldn't have known." An unspoken understanding lingered between them. Malachi gave a subtle head nod toward Bianca in the car, beckoning her closer.

As they walked side by side toward the tombstone, Malachi recounted the security officer's words. "Did you catch what the security said?" he asked, his voice a mixture of curiosity and concern.

Bianca nodded, her expression turning thoughtful. "Yeah, I heard. Do you think your father was murdered?"

The question lingered in the chilly air, and the first person to come to Malachi's mind was Peter. He considered the implications silently before voicing his thoughts.

Their footsteps echoed softly as they moved deeper into the cemetery's embrace.

"Well, if he was, it would be a good thing —well, not a good thing," Malachi said, his voice trailing off. Bianca patted his shoulder gently and replied, "I know what you mean."

Miguel was already there, nervously shifting his feet in the grass.

Malachi joined him, and they both looked at their mother.

There, their mother knelt by the tombstone, wearing a flowing white dress that cascaded elegantly around her. Her round glasses framed her eyes, and her white dreadlocks were adorned with silver clips that sparkled in the moonlight.

A sparking V-shaped choker wrapped around her neck, complementing her dark skin as she knelt quietly, the soft glow of the moon illuminating her presence.

Her presence was both commanding and serene.

Touching the tombstone, Malachi felt a chill.

He could almost hear his father's voice, a whisper carried on the wind.

"Goodbye, my love.

You were my rock, my guiding star. Rest now; we will carry on your legacy."

Their mother's voice, strong and clear, broke through the silence. Her tears glimmered, but her voice remained steady.

"Our sons are here, strong and brave.

They will make you proud.

 Looking up at the night sky.

"Father, he did his best. Embrace his spirit and guide him home." Her voice trembled with conviction.

She kissed her fingers and softly touched the tombstone. After a quick tap on the grave.

Miguel gave Malachi a nod, and then their mother turned.

Her eyes lit up with excitement when she saw them. They walked to her, each stepping to one of her sides.

She wrapped her arms around them, pulling them close.

Mrs. Shaka caught sight of Bianca and immediately moved toward her with enthusiasm.

"Hey, girl!" she exclaimed, pulling her into a warm hug.

As they embraced, they exchanged heartfelt sentiments about how wonderful it was to see each other. Stepping back, Mrs. Shaka gave Bianca an admiring look, her eyes full of warmth. "Oh my, look at you, getting all fabulous," she teased with a gentle, knowing smile. "You're truly a goddess!"

Blushing and smiling, Bianca said, "Stop it!" Meanwhile, Malachi sneaked a glance at Bianca's body before quickly looking away. Miguel caught the whole thing and started chuckling.

Mrs. Shaka's eyes then fell on Bianca's dress. "This dress is stunning! Where did you get it?"

Bianca beamed, a hint of pride in her voice, "I made it myself. It's tough finding anything that fits these hips just right." As she said this, she playfully flexed her leg, showing off her handiwork.

Mrs. Shaka raised an eyebrow in surprise. "I didn't know you had such a talent! Anytime I need a dress, I'm calling you."

Then, with heartfelt sincerity, Mrs. Shaka thanked Bianca for being there and supporting her boys.

"It's no problem at all," Bianca replied, touched.

Mrs. Shaka told Bianca, "You're family now. If you need anything, don't hesitate to call. Need a room? Just come over, alright?"

Bianca felt a surge of emotion, touched by the sense of belonging and acceptance.

The brothers exchanged warm smiles, a silent communication of shared affection and understanding. Malachi lingered for a moment, his gaze softening as it settled on Bianca.

He took in her beauty, the gentle curve of her smile illuminating the space around them.

"How are you two doing ?" Mrs Shaka asked, her voice laced with genuine concern.

Miguel, ever the smooth talker, grinned and replied, "We're good Ma.

How was the flight?"

"Exhausting," she admitted, a chuckle escaping her lips.

"But worth it."

She gave their shoulders a warm squeeze and laughed, "Damn, look at you two! So, where've you been growing… or going?"

Miguel, feeling a bit annoyed, said, "Ma, that's not even funny." She shrugged it off and said, "Oh, hush up anyway! How've you two been?"

Malachi, ever the dutiful son, answered first.

"I've been researching a few schools, Ma," he said, his voice filled with determination.

"There's one I have my eye on to pursue a career in medicine."

Miguel, ever the carefree spirit, shrugged. "Nothing much, just chilling." He knew that wasn't entirely true, but he didn't want to worry her with the details.

"Nothing?" she echoed, a hint of amusement in her voice.

Malachi couldn't help but think that if he had said that, she would have been at his neck.

"Speaking of nothing," she continued, her tone softening.

"Have you heard the rumors surrounding your father's death?"

Miguel sighed with resignation. "Unfortunately, yeah."

Bianca glanced at Malachi, who briefly met her eyes before looking away, their silent exchange speaking volumes.

"For now, let's set that aside," Miguel said, shifting his gaze to Malachi.

"He did the eulogy, Ma."

Her eyes widened, and a soft smile spread across her face. "Malachi, you did?"

"Yeah," he said, his voice a little sheepish.

"Peter wanted me to read one he wrote," he said thoughtfully, shaking his head. "Honestly, it was a load of nonsense."

Miguel's brow furrowed in disbelief as he listened. Finally, he shook his head and uttered a dumbfounded, "What?"

Their mother sighed, shaking her head.

"Why am I not surprised?"

"Speaking of Peter," she said, her voice light.

"Your father never liked him."

Their laughter echoed through the room, a sound that filled the space where their father had once stood.

"We know, Ma," they said in unison.

Miguel then added, "Hey, ma you know that Gramps wants to see us tomorrow."

Their mother looked startled.

Malachi noticed and started to ask why, but she cut him off.

"Just be careful, okay?"

Malachi's eyebrows shot up.

Why that reaction?"

"Why did he have to die?" Miguel finally asked, his voice cracking.

His mother's expression softened, a flicker of sadness passing over her face.

She gently pulled him into a hug, his head resting against her shoulder.

"Sometimes, darling," she whispered, her voice tender and thoughtful, "the most beautiful souls leave this world so we can hold them closer in our hearts."

Turning to Bianca, she sought a connection. "Isn't that right, Bianca?" she asked gently.

Bianca nodded, a soft "Mhmm" slipping from her lips, her eyes reflecting mutual understanding. Their mother chuckled softly, her laughter a brief, uplifting melody amid their shared sorrow.

Malachi watched them, a quiet understanding settling over him.

He walked towards his father's tombstone, the words etched in stone a constant reminder of his loss.

He read them aloud, a whisper barely audible above the rustle of leaves: "Death is mankind's greatest gift from God, the ultimate liberation from the chains of mortality."

His mother came up behind him, her hand resting lightly on his shoulder.

She gazed at the tombstone, a hint of steel in her eyes.

"Travel safe, Dad," Malachi whispered his voice a blend of deep grief and unexpected peace.

Beside him, Bianca gently rubbed his back, her touch offering quiet comfort in the solemn moment.

To be continued....

CHAPTER 5- FOUNDING FATHER

The sleek black sedan glided to a stop before the gates nestled into the mountainside.

As the driver, a lively Indian man with a friendly smile, expertly parked, Miguel leaned back in the plush seat, grateful. "Thanks, man, you're a lifesaver," he drawled.

Malachi, still chewing gum, tapped the driver and slipped a bill into his hand. "Keep the change, alright," he said with a nod.

"Much appreciated," the driver replied warmly.

Stepping out, Miguel stretched against the fading sunlight, while Malachi followed with precise movements.

"You know there's a perfectly good door on your side," Miguel teased. Malachi smirked, "Nah, I just like a good entrance."

As they made their way to the security booth, Malachi noticed it was empty. "Where's the guard?" he muttered, puzzled.

Just then, the smaller gate clicked open, and he turned to see Miguel spinning a key on his finger. "What, I got a key, don't you?" Miguel grinned.

Malachi rolled his eyes, giving Miguel a light shove. Stepping inside, they were enveloped by the mansion's grandeur, hidden within the mountain.

Elegant and timeless, its soaring ceilings and crystal chandeliers bathed everything in a golden glow, whispering the secrets of the Shaka clan that it sheltered.

Paintings and family portraits, whispering tales of history and legacy.

In the hallway, illuminated by the sun's warm embrace through a large window, sat their cousin Eli at a grand piano.

Clad entirely in white, his locs were elegantly tied into a bun, secured by a white headband that added to his composed demeanor.

Yet, there was something hauntingly vacant about him, a deadened vibe that lingered especially in his eyes, which seemed to carry the weight of unspoken burdens.

He looked up from the piano keys, his eyes twinkling with mischief, and said, "Oh hey guys ?"

The cousins greeted each other with a firm dap, a gesture underscored by the rich history they shared.

Among them, Eli stood out as the youngest of all the grandchildren—a fact that had shaped much of his experience within the family.

Often surrounded by older cousins, Eli had grown up absorbing their stories and wisdom, his youthful perspective offering a fresh lens that occasionally disrupted the status quo.

Yet, there was a quiet resilience about him, a maturity that belied his years, earned from navigating the shadows of those who came before him.

"Whatcha up to, man?" Miguel asked, his voice tinged with curiosity.

Eli sighed dramatically, "Stuck in piano lessons.

Can't a brother catch a break?"

Malachi snorted, "Sucks to be you.

But we're about to head upstairs, you'll be fine."

He gently pushed Miguel towards the elevator, his eyes flickering with a hidden agenda.

Eli, his gaze fixed on the piano, gave them a thumbs-up.

In the heart of the grand mansion, the unidentical twins, Malachi and Miguel, brought a vibrant energy to the old halls. Malachi, with his keen observational skills, complemented Miguel's boundless imagination and exuberance.

As they moved through the corridors, the maids continued their tasks, nodding at the familiar sight of the energetic duo. The sounds of their cousins playing above blended with their footsteps, muffled by the plush carpet, as they ascended the grand staircase together.

At the summit, the majestic mahogany door awaited them, a symbol of the mysteries hidden beyond.

The guards, in their pristine white attire, subtly shifted in acknowledgment of the twins' infectious spirit—a reminder of adventure thriving within the mansion's austere grandeur.

In this realm of tradition, it was the spirited divergence of Malachi and Miguel that infused life and wonder into every corner, transforming the mundane into the extraordinary. Malachi exhaled a deep breath, the tension evident in his posture.

Miguel glanced over, a trace of amusement in his eyes. "What, are you nervous?" he asked, a subtle smile playing at the corners of his lips.

Nearby, one guard briefly looked at his colleague, who responded with a slight shake of his head, communicating silently with a practiced ease.

Malachi scoffed, "Who, me? Nah."

Miguel gestured toward the door, a playful glint in his eye. "So, Enter, then."

Malachi shot back, "You got legs too," but before he could react, Miguel gave him a playful shove, sending him stumbling towards the door.

The guards, stone-faced sentinels, opened the door for them, their movements precise and efficient.

The room was vast, furnished with opulent extravagance. A massive bed, draped in rich fabrics, dominated the space. Behind a large desk, sitting in a black suit, was their grandfather.

Long, white locs tumbled down his shoulders, framing a face softened by a full white beard.

One amber-brown eye, bright and keen, peered over a stack of papers. He looked up as they entered.

"Look who it is," he said, a smile playing on his lips. "My boys." Miguel nudged Malachi. "See? He's not mad." They settled into the chairs opposite the desk.

Malachi followed closely, his tone a mix of concern and gentle admonishment, "Gramps! What do you think you're doing?"

Gramps looked up, eyes warming as he greeted, "What's up, Migz?

"I'm chilling, Gramps," he replied with a smile.

Turning to Malachi, the grandfather gave a playful nod, asking, "How's it going, little man?"

Malachi, with a faint grin, responded, "I don't appreciate being called that."
Laughter erupted among them.

"Boy, am I happy to see you boys," he said, his eyes twinkling with a lifetime of memories.

"So tell me, why do I have to send for you boys to see your faces?" he asked, his voice carrying both the burden of time and the sweetness of familial bonds.

Silence enveloped the room. Malachi's stoic facade showed a flicker of regret, while Miguel, usually expressive, found his words tangled in emotion.

Seeing their struggle, the old man sighed with a tender smile.

"Ah, boys, life pulls us in many directions, but this old heart always yearns to your faces."

Grandpa extended his hands.

He took theirs in a firm grasp, gently squeezing as his thumb traced soothing circles on the back of their hands, his gaze steady and reassuring.

"How was the funeral?"

Miguel hesitated, his voice tinged with discomfort.

"It was…umm…" He glanced at Malachi, seeking silent confirmation.

Malachi nodded, his expression tight. "It was alright."

Grandpa's eyes sharpened, his gaze piercing, a seasoned warrior assessing the battlefield.

"Peter was there?"

Malachi nodded, his gaze fixed on the floor.

"Yup," he mumbled, his voice barely audible, though his expression hinted that wasn't all.

Grandpa, sensing the omission, pressed further, his voice a low rumble. "Alright, what did he do?"

Malachi faltered, his eyes widening in alarm. "Huh?"

Grandpa's gaze turned knowing, his voice laced with a touch of amusement.

"Huh? That's what people say before they lie."

To be continued...

CHAPTER 6- NEW ERA

Miguel turned towards Grandpa, his voice tinged with a mix of frustration and discomfort.

"Well of one Peter came late, and Malachi had to deliver the eulogy."

Malachi, looking a bit pale, was too nervous to tell Gramps the truth.

Miguel leaned forward in his chair. Feet, awaiting Grandpa's reaction.

Grandpa's sharp eyes, filled with the wisdom of countless years, settled on Malachi.

He uttered a thoughtful "Hmm," before breaking into a knowing smile.

"I'm not even surprised.

Your father was Enoch, after all."

Miguel seized the opportunity to tease, his tone turning playful.

"So Gramps, Dad was your favorite, wasn't he ?"

Grandpa snorted loudly, flapping his lips in a mock show of indignation.

"No, I didn't have favorites.

I love all my kids equally."

Malachi couldn't hold back his smirk, his skepticism evident.

"Sure," he replied, drawing out the word.

"Boy!" he exclaimed, the word dripping with affectionate reprimand.

Laughter filled the room, a rare moment of joy amidst the somber occasion.

But the laughter was abruptly cut short when Grandpa started to cough, a deep, wrenching sound that seemed to shake his entire frail form.

Malachi's smile vanished as he watched Grandpa intently, his concern growing with each ragged breath.

Grandpa's hand, trembling slightly, covered his mouth.

When he withdrew it, he stared at his palm for a long while, his expression darkening.

Malachi's senses picked up the faint, metallic scent of blood lingering in the air.

His heart pounded as his eyes met Grandpa's, a silent exchange of shared worry.

Miguel looked over with concern etched across his face and asked, "Gramps, you good?"

Grandpa waved his hand dismissively, his voice gruff but reassuring.

"Yeah, I'll live."

Yet, Malachi felt a deep unease.

His senses, always sharp, were picking up subtle signs that contradicted Grandpa's words.

The slightly sour smell of sweat that clung to Grandpa's clothes, the faint pallor of his skin, and the slight tremor in his voice all painted a different picture.

"Now, here's the deal," Grandpa said, his voice dropping to a serious tone. He shifted in his chair, locking his hands on the desk, his intense gaze locking onto Malachi and Miguel, making their stomachs clench.

"I need you two to attend a soiree on my behalf. You must represent our side of the clan."

"My legs... well, they're not what they used to be," he said, and Grandpa chuckled, patting his leg.

Malachi, already wary of the prospect, frowned.

"A dance party, Gramps? Why?"

Grandpa chuckled softly.

"It's a ball celebrating our country's rise as a powerful nation, marking a significant turning point in our history."

A victory, you might say."

He paused, letting the significance of the words hang in the air. "And it has to be the two of you."

Miguel, ever the eager one, grinned. "Gramps, you don't need to explain further.

We're in."

Malachi, however, remained hesitant. "But why us?" he pressed, his brow furrowed.
Grandpa's eyes narrowed, a spark of anticipation gleaming within them.

"Because," he said, his voice steady but laced with urgency, "I need you both at this soirée. It's essential.

There are critical matters to address and important connections to forge, and I have complete confidence in you two to navigate it wisely. This isn't just a party; it's a strategic gathering. I'm counting on you to be my eyes and ears, ensuring everything unfolds as it should. Consider this your initiation into the family's future."

His voice dropped to a near whisper. "This is a crucial social engagement, and your presence is vital to the family's success."

He paused, his eyes drifting toward the window, taking in the estate's expanse.

"Take Deon with you," Grandpa said. Malachi looked up at him, questioning, "What?"

Don't want to give him another reason to hate you."

Malachi looked at Gramps with a surprised expression, eyebrows raised slightly in intrigue.

"Oh, you knew?"

Gramps chuckled, the sound rich with age and wisdom. "I may be old, but I ain't cold."

Miguel barked out a laugh, gesturing with his hand in confusion.

"What does that even mean?"

Gramps looked at him with twinkling eyes. "When you grow some more, you'll understand."

Then Miguel leaned in, his voice a conspiratorial whisper. "Talk to Mal about growing."

Malachi's brow furrowed in confusion. "What?"

Miguel hesitated, a nervous chuckle escaping his lips.

"Hm? Did you say something?" he deflected, trying to mask his earlier comment.

Shuffling closer, he lowered his voice, his words deliberate and heavy with meaning.

"This is more than just attending an event. The island needs to witness the emerging generation of Shaka's.

Our people are searching for hope, and they need to see you both—our future—standing proud and strong."
Grandpa's gaze was intense as he spoke. "This is about a new era for enlightened humans who will carry on our legacy. Your presence symbolizes unity and strength, proving our spirit thrives through you."

"This goes beyond any individual—it's about our future as a united people. And that, my children, starts with you."

A hint of mischief sparkled in his eyes as he glanced at Malachi.
"You can even bring your 'friend' along," Grandpa suggested, his tone loaded with unspoken meanings.

Malachi's brows furrowed. "I don't have a girlfriend," he replied, bewilderment lacing his voice.

Miguel snapped his fingers, a grin of realization spreading across his face. "Oh, you mean Bianca!" he said with a teasing gleam in his eyes.

Malachi's cheeks flushed with a mix of frustration and embarrassment. "She's just a friend, not my girlfriend," he insisted, the words tumbling out defensively.

Grandpa's smirk broadened, his voice rich with sarcasm. "Just a friend, huh? And I suppose that makes me a rocket scientist."

Before Malachi could respond, Grandpa's expression softened, and his tone turned wistful.

"You know, it reminds me of when your Grandma and I…" Grandpa started with a nostalgic smile.

Malachi quickly interjected, "Grandpa, we get it. You and Grandma were young and reckless. Spare us the details."

Grandpa deflated slightly, rubbing his beard thoughtfully. "Well, alright, alright," he murmured. "I just thought I'd share a few stories, maybe put you in on the game a bit."

As his words trailed off, a heavy silence settled in. Malachi stared at his feet, feeling a knot of tension forming in his chest.

Miguel, ever the quieter one, sat beside him, his eyes downcast.

Finally, Grandpa broke the silence, his voice thick with emotion.

Gramps looked up, his voice heavy with emotion. "I miss my son.

 I miss him terribly," he murmured, as a tear slowly snaked down his cheek.

Malachi and Miguel exchanged a glance.

There was a shared understanding in their eyes, a silent acknowledgment of the elephant in the room, the grief that lingered like a heavy fog.

Miguel reached for Grandpa's hand.

"We miss him too, Gramps," he murmured, his voice barely audible.

Malachi nodded, his voice catching in his throat.

He wished he could say more, could offer his grandfather some comfort, but the words wouldn't come.

All he could do was sit there, in the quiet, with the weight of their shared loss pressing down on them.

To be continued....

CHAPTER 7- GANG

The fluorescent lights hummed above the worn courtroom table.

Malachi, Miguel, their mother—a baby nestled against her chest—and the lawyer sat facing each other.

The lawyer, a bald man with a neatly trimmed goatee, sported a surprisingly loud striped suit.

"Thank you all again," he began, his voice smooth and practiced.

His eyes, however, lingered a little too long on their mother's face, a subtle, unsettling smile playing on his lips—a clear breach of professional decorum that didn't go unnoticed by the sharp-eyed brothers.

She shifted uncomfortably, her hand instinctively moving to adjust the baby's blanket.

Miguel cleared his throat, a sharp sound that cut through the lawyer's practiced charm. Both brothers leaned forward, their attention suddenly laser-focused on the proceedings, their protective instincts already on high alert due to the lawyer's inappropriate behavior.

The lawyer, momentarily flustered by Miguel's interruption and the brothers' intense scrutiny, continued, "Regarding the JDF enrollment... if the brothers choose to participate, they will be granted full access to Mr. Shaka's research."

Miguel scoffed. "Yeah, that's never going to happen," he said, his tone dismissive.

Malachi chuckled, a low rumble in his chest.

"Very well," the lawyer said, smoothly recovering. "Moving on.

The estate will be divided as follows: your mother will receive fifty percent of the financial assets.

The remaining fifty percent will be divided equally between the two of you. Miguel, you will inherit the Audi R8."

Miguel's eyes widened, a grin splitting his face.

He practically bounced in his seat, a stark contrast to his usual reserved demeanor. The sheer childish glee was palpable.

Malachi, his hand at his jaw, side-eyed his childish brother, a hint of amusement and exasperation playing across his features.

"Malachi," the lawyer continued, "you will inherit the secluded house in Blue Mountain."

Malachi's eyes went wide as he heard the news.

"What?" he exclaimed.

Suddenly, Miguel reached over and gave Malachi's shoulder a playful shake, laughing heartily.

Malachi looked over to see his mother smiling warmly at him.

She raised her eyebrows expectantly, and Malachi found himself nodding in response, still processing the unexpected inheritance.

Then came the reading of the personal effects.

Their mother received a collection of antique books, each inscribed with loving messages from their father; a hand-painted watercolor of a mountain landscape, strikingly similar to the view from the Blue Mountain house; and a small, worn leather-bound journal filled with his private thoughts and sketches.

The lawyer's eyebrows rose; even the brothers exchanged surprised glances.

Malachi, staring at the items listed, felt a sudden, overwhelming wave of realization.

He hadn't known his father had been this... sentimental.

The sheer volume and personal nature of the items suggested a depth of wealth and emotion far beyond what he'd ever imagined.

The lawyer's surprise, and even his own, spoke volumes about just how much their father had truly loved their mother.
As Mr. Patrick sifted through the last few pages of the will, he tried to lighten the mood, hoping everyone would forget his earlier slip-up.

"Looks like you've all hit the jackpot!" he joked, flashing a grin.

But then, unable to resist going completely off-track, he turned to their mom with a playful glint in his eye. "Well, looks like you're a free agent now, huh? No more Mr. Shaka tying you down," he said with a wink.

Both brothers, trying to process the lawyer's bold and out-of-place comment, leaned their heads to the side in perfect sync, eyebrows raised as if silently saying, "Did he just go there?"

Instantly, the atmosphere shifted.

The brothers stood up simultaneously, a wave of protective outrage emanating from them, their earlier amusement completely gone.

Their mother, with the baby, still cradled on her hip, rose calmly but firmly, addressing the lawyer with cool courtesy.

"Okay, Mr. Patrick, thank you so much for everything.

Have a blessed day."

She offered her hand. As Mr. Patrick reached for it, Miguel cut him off.

A fiery orange glow erupted from Miguel's hand as he grasped the lawyer's.

A high-pitched scream ripped through the air as Mr. Patrick's eyes widened, his hand recoiling instantly. The searing heat was palpable; the smell of burning flesh filled the air.

He frantically rubbed his hand, his face contorted in agony, a low, guttural moan escaping his lips.
Miguel, keeping his voice calm but with a hint of underlying menace, said, "We appreciate your help."

The lawyer winced in agony as Miguel's fiery touch scorched his flesh, leaving an angry red mark on his palm.

Wisps of smoke curled up from his blistered skin, and he fought to contain his anguished cries, not wanting to draw further attention to the situation.

With Miguel and their mother already leaving the room, Malachi's glare, cold and heavy, lingered on the Lawyer.

It was a look that could freeze blood, a death stare that spoke of simmering rage.

Inside, Malachi was a storm brewing, his fists clenched, every muscle coiled tight, yearning to unleash the fury building within.

He imagined the lawyer cowering beneath his blows, a pathetic rabbit caught in the jaws of a wolf.

The lawyer, sensing the predator's gaze, remained frozen in place, a single bead of sweat rolling down his temple.

Then, from the doorway, his mother's voice called out, "Malachi," snapping his attention back to her with an urgent head jerk.

Her eyes said it all: let it go.

Malachi gave the lawyer one last glare and with a hint of sarcasm in his voice said, "Have a blessed day," before turning on his heel and walking out.

Outside the courthouse, the family regrouped.

The baby stirred, letting out a tiny wail that their mother quickly soothed with gentle rocking.

Miguel turned to her, hesitating for just a moment. "Ma?" he began.

"Yeah?" she replied, focused on the baby.

"Gramps wants us to attend this dance party on his behalf."

A soft smile played across her lips. "Aw, he loves you guys."

Meanwhile, Malachi crouched beside his sister, was busy pulling faces that sent her into fits of laughter, momentarily forgetting the world around them.

"So, when is it?" their mother asked.

Malachi checked the time, a grin tugging at his lips.

"Not too far from now," he said. Just then, his phone buzzed.

"Here he is now," he murmured, bringing his wrist to his ear as Miguel leaned in.

The vibrant voice of their grandfather burst through the speaker.

"Hey, what's up, man? Hope you guys haven't forgotten about me."

"Nah, Nah, just taking care of something with Mom," Malachi assured.

"Oh yeah? Let me talk to her."

Their mother took the call, her voice softening. "Hey, Mr. Shaka."

"Hey, Maria, how's it going?"

"I'm good. How about you?"

"I'm not a hundred percent, but I'm holding on."

"That's good to hear."

"Hey, I'm going to steal your boys for a night, all right?"

She chuckled. "That's fine. Do me a favor and keep them!"

The brothers exchanged mock indignant looks, which only added to the laughter.

"How's my little princess?" Gramps inquired.

"She's all right, acting like she's all grown up already."

"Heh heh, they don't stay small for long."

"You're not wrong," she said softly. "All right, I'm going to let you go."

"Take care."

As the call ended, their mother kissed their foreheads, whispering, "Take care, love you."

She walked toward her car, Malachi waving enthusiastically to his sister. "Bye, Malia!"

Miguel, grinning, jested, "You're a nice guy, you know."

Malachi shot him a mock glare. "What's that supposed to mean?"

Miguel chuckled, "You don't like anybody. Glad you like your sister."

"Negro ain't she your sister too".

They exchanged playful shoves just as a BMW pulled up beside them.

Bianca leaned out, disappointment clear as the boy's mother's jeep passed by, honking a farewell.

"Oh man, I missed her." She sighed.

The brothers hopped into the car, exchanging fist bumps with Bianca. "So, how'd it go?" she asked.

Miguel in the back seat stretched his arm along the chair, a contented smile stretching across his face.

"Let's just say we're rich."

"Weren't you guys already filthy rich?" Bianca teased.

Miguel laughed, nodding.

"Yeah, but now we're even richer."

Malachi chimed in, "Alright, how do you feel about going to a dance party?" Before he said anything, he was wondering how to ask her.

He wanted to sound cool, but his nerves were getting to him.

He fumbled with his words, "So, uh, I was thinking... maybe... you know, we could..."

He stopped himself, realizing how ridiculous he sounded.

Taking a deep breath, he tried again.

"Would you, like, be interested in going to a dance party...?"

Bianca raised an eyebrow, mischief in her eyes.

"Dance party? With you?"

"Yeah, with us," Malachi confirmed.

Bianca considered the invitation, her eyebrows rising slightly with amusement.

"Hmmmm, okay," she replied, a playful glint in her eyes.

A silent exchange passed between the brothers, a shared look of relief and satisfaction.

Miguel broke the moment with a grin, leaning back into his seat as he remarked, "Well, that went well."

Bianca leaned back against the headrest, a tired smile hinting at the corners of her mouth.

"I just got back from school and honestly, I need a break," she confessed.

"Plus, spending time with the best people in my life? Yeah, I need that."

As she spoke, Malachi pretended to brush invisible dust from his pants, trying to play it cool.

From the back seat, Miguel watched his brother's antics with a smirk and chimed in, "Well, for one, I'm grateful we've got a ride to go.

Beats having security stalking us any day."

Bianca chuckled, shifting the car into drive.

"We just need Dante to come back, and then the gang will be complete," she said, a twinkle in her eye as the car smoothly pulled away, carrying them toward their next adventure.

To be continued….

CHAPTER 8-

PEOPLE PERSON

Malachi checked himself out in the mirror, admiring the pop of his red suit against the black buttoned undershirt he wore.

His white locs were adorned with gold cuffs, glinting under the light and adding an extra flair to his confident appearance.

He stared at himself, shaking his head with a mix of disbelief and determination.

"The things I do for family," he muttered, reminding himself of the importance of the occasion ahead.

The vibrant colors and the gold accents in his hair weren't just for looks—they symbolized his connection to those he cared about, a reminder of why he was stepping into this moment with pride.

A cool cross necklace hung around his neck, adding the final touch to his look.

He reached up, gathering his thick locs into a neat, high ponytail, the dark strands catching the light as he secured them with a simple black band.

The ponytail added a touch of formality to his already polished appearance, balancing the bold lines of his suit with a touch of his style.

He adjusted the collar of his shirt, then ran a hand down the front of his jacket, feeling the smooth, luxurious fabric.

Malachi took out his phone, murmuring to himself, "Let's see where this girl is," as he scrolled through his contacts to find Bianca.

Just as he was about to call her, a loud banging erupted at his door, interrupting his thoughts.

"What the hell?" he muttered, striding over to the door.

He swung it open to reveal Deon, halfway through buttoning his sleeve, a grin plastered on his face.

"You ready? It's starting in a few minutes," Deon announced, oblivious to the impatience in Malachi's eyes.

"Deon, first off, don't bang on my door like that," Malachi replied with a sigh, attempting to keep his annoyance in check.

"And second, I'm not going with you."

Deon raised an eyebrow, curious. "Oh? Who's taking you then?"

Without another word, Malachi simply smiled a subtle quirk of mischief in his expression, and gently closed the door.

Malachi dialed Bianca's number, listening to the ringing that seemed to stretch longer with each second.

Just as his annoyance began to peak, she finally picked up.

"Don't you know to answer on the first ring?" he teased, a smirk playing on his lips.

"Shut up, Mal.

Can't you see I'm driving?" Bianca shot back, her playful irritation coming through clearly.

He laughed, a deep, genuine sound. "I'm just messing with you.

How far out are you?"

"Look out the window. I'm right outside," she responded confidently.

"Already? Alright then," Malachi replied, hanging up with a smile.

He moved to the door, anticipation quickening his steps.

Just as he went to grab the knob, the door swung open and there was Miguel, decked out in a white suit.

His blonde locs framed his amber-brown skin, standing out against Malachi's cool almond complexion. "Look at that, we're in sync," Miguel said with a chuckle, dropping his hand.

Malachi spun Miguel around, gently steering him toward the hall.

"Yeah, yeah, B's here," he said with a mischievous grin.

"Let's get outta here before Deon finds us and starts nagging me again," Malachi muttered, pulling his hood low over his head.

As they walked, Miguel slowed down to match Malachi's pace and glanced over. "What's the deal with you and Deon?" he asked. "You guys used to be close."

Malachi shrugged, trying to look casual. "I just don't like him anymore."

Miguel sighed. "That's a bit unfair, you know." He shoved Miguel hard, sending him stumbling down the hall.

Malachi didn't look back, his footsteps echoing as he disappeared around a corner.

As the duo exited the grand mansion, its towering façade looming majestically against the night sky, they were met with the familiar sight of Deon casually leaning against the side wall, his attention seemingly absorbed by the glow of his phone screen.

His posture was relaxed, one foot propped against the wall, but there was an air of restlessness about him.

Malachi, already descending the steps, paused mid-stride and glanced over at Deon with a mix of amusement and exasperation.

Deon's presence was as predictable as it was enigmatic, especially when there were possibilities of mischief involved.

Deon, sensing the gaze, looked up from his phone, offering a lopsided grin that spoke of mischief well-planned.

Malachi, with a sudden playful impulse, gave Miguel a gentle push toward Bianca's sleek, obsidian-black car parked nearby.

Miguel stumbled good-naturedly, grinning as he opened the door and hopped into the back seat.

Malachi followed swiftly, sliding into the front passenger seat beside Bianca with an easy grin.

Bianca turned toward them, arching a perfectly shaped eyebrow at their impromptu switch.

"Hey," she exclaimed, mock indignation in her voice.

"You guys that happy to see me?"

Caught off guard, Miguel and Malachi exchanged a quick, comically shocked look before bursting into laughter.

The shared glance conveyed years of friendship and countless shared misadventures.

Malachi was the first to regain his composure, shaking his head with an amused smirk.

"No," he replied with faux seriousness, crossing his arms as he settled comfortably into the seat.

"But yes, of course!" Miguel chimed in loudly from the back, exaggerating his enthusiasm with a wide grin.

Bianca started the car with a flick of her wrist, a nonchalant "whatever" escaping her lips as she did.

Her eyes darted to Malachi in the back seat.

"Mal, what's that address?" she asked, glancing at him through the rearview mirror.

Malachi leaned forward, handing over his phone with the GPS map displayed.

The rhythmic hum of the city filled the car as they journeyed through the maze of streets, the Pegasus Hotel drawing nearer.

Its towering, art deco façade loomed as they arrived, the building's lights casting shimmering reflections onto their windshield.

She parked and turned off the engine with precision, her smile warm as she faced her companions.

Miguel, the joker of the group, nudged Malachi's shoulder, a playful grin stretching across his face.

Malachi shot him a look, eyebrow cocked, as if to say, "Really?" The camaraderie was palpable in Bianca's amused chuckle as she slipped free of her seatbelt.

Right on cue, her door swung open, revealing the valet—a tall guy in a sharp black and red uniform, with skin like golden sand.

With an easy smile, he offered his hand and said, "May I help you out?"

Bianca laughed, taking the valet's hand. "You scared me for a second!" she said, looking stunning in her black TS Mermaid sequin gown with a champagne satin bodice, long sleeves, and pearl details.
The valet grinned apologetically and said, "Sorry about that. I'm just a gentleman at heart, can't help myself."

Meanwhile, Malachi glanced at Miguel sitting in the back seat, and Miguel just shrugged, amused by the whole interaction.

Malachi stepped out, his eyes narrowing as he regarded the valet with a mix of curiosity and skepticism.

The valet's voice was smooth, his words wrapped in a polite drawl.

"My apologies, light skin, but as I told you I'm a gentleman at heart."

Bianca felt at ease again, her wary chuckle softening as she adjusted her dress.

As the brothers headed towards the entrance, the valet greeted Malachi with a friendly fist bump.

"How's it going, my guy?" he said with a casual nod.

Malachi stepped around the valet, not breaking his stride as he heard Bianca calling out to him.

She quickly went after him, trying to catch up.

Miguel, lingering momentarily, turned to the valet with an apologetic half-smile, hands raised as if to make peace.

"My bad, bro, he's not a people person."

The valet glanced over his shoulder at Malachi and Bianca as they navigated through the crowd gathered at the entrance.

Walking hand in hand, Bianca playfully poked Malachi's head, scolding him with a teasing smile.

Chewing gum nonchalantly, the valet said, "Is that so?" with a glint in his eyes that suggested an understanding beyond words.

Miguel couldn't shake the uneasy feeling as he glanced at the valet, who seemed to take notice of his suspicion.

With an almost playful smirk, the valet gave Miguel a friendly pat on the shoulder.

"Enjoy the show," he said, the corner of his mouth twitching up just a bit too knowingly.

"I've got a hunch it's going to be memorable."

That sneaky smile of his lingered, making Miguel wonder what exactly he might be hinting at.

Miguel started making his way towards the entrance but couldn't help glancing back at the valet one last time.

Just then, he heard Malachi call out to him from inside.

Turning his focus back, he saw Bianca waving him over with a welcoming smile.

With a small nod, Miguel shook off his uneasy thoughts and headed inside to join them.

To be continued...

CHAPTER 9- ROYALTIES

Malachi stepped into the bustling lobby of the Pegasus Hotel, the excited whispers of the crowd washing over him.

Internally, he struggled with the overwhelming presence of people and the unwanted spotlight that seemed to follow him. He despised the grandeur and pretense, his jaw tight with displeasure.

As he and Miguel navigated the lavish space, guests in designer attire began to part, their expressions a mix of admiration and curiosity.

A hush fell over the room, and murmurs of *"It's Malachi and Miguel!"* rippled through the crowd. The way people straightened up revealed their awareness of the brothers' influence, heightening Malachi's discomfort as he braced for the event ahead.

The murmurs intensified, a low hum of anticipation building as all eyes followed Malachi and Miguel to their table.

The brothers' presence was not merely their own; it was intertwined with their father's illustrious legacy, a legacy that held the room captive.

In this setting, their anonymity was nonexistent. They were not just individuals but embodiments of a powerful lineage, their very presence commanding both attention and reverence.

Even young boys, eyes wide with awe, reached out for autographs, clutching tattered pieces of paper like treasures.

Malachi offered a quick nod and a practiced smile to each outstretched hand, while Bianca discreetly guided him through the throng, ensuring they made their way with the grace befitting their status.

They finally reached the ballroom doors, the music, and laughter from within spilling out into the foyer.

As they entered, the scene shifted from youthful exuberance to hushed respect.

The air hummed with a mix of polished wood and faint floral arrangements, underscored by the melodic strains of a string quartet playing softly in the corner.

A sea of well-dressed dignitaries began to gravitate towards them, each wearing expressions that skillfully balanced sympathy and diplomatic decorum.

Malachi felt the uncomfortable weight of their gazes, a sensation akin to being pinned under a microscope.

Leading this formidable group was Senator Jackson, renowned for his polished demeanor as much as his political acumen.

He extended a hand warmly, his voice a well-rehearsed, low murmur.
"Malachi, Miguel," the senator said, his voice heavy with feigned sympathy. "I was deeply saddened to hear of your father's passing.

He was an extraordinary man, and his legacy will resonate for generations." He shook their hands with an overly firm grip, attempting to convey strength and solidarity.

The senator spoke broadly about the significant opportunities emerging in Jamaica, then proposed an alliance with the Shaka clan—an offer carefully tailored to Malachi and Miguel, whose disinterest in politics was well known.

He emphasized that with other politicians already aligning with influential clans, he needed to solidify his position by partnering with a leading family like theirs.

This alliance, he suggested, would foster mutual benefits and enhance their collective influence in the region, regardless of Malachi and Miguel's apparent disinterest.

Malachi's discomfort grew as he sensed the hidden motives and urgency behind the senator's words, realizing they were stepping into a dangerous game of alliances and betrayals.

His sincerity served as an unspoken bridge, connecting him with a genuine appreciation for those around him.

Noticing the imperceptible tension rising from Malachi, Bianca subtly edged closer, her presence a calming influence.

Her hand found its way to his side, delivering a gentle but unmistakable pinch meant to urge caution.

She turned towards him, whispering just loud enough for only him to hear, "Do you want to give the family a bad name?"

With Bianca's subtle nudge, Malachi managed to rein in his unease, choosing to engage more civilly with those who had gathered to pay their respects.

As the crowd slowly dispersed, the brothers finally found a moment of calm, settling at a nearby table.

As they relaxed, an announcer stepped to the podium, their voice resonating with authority throughout the room.

"Ladies and gentlemen, may I have your attention, please?

It is with great honor that we welcome Malachi and Miguel of the esteemed Shaka clan to our gathering this evening.

We extend our deepest condolences for their recent loss and express our sincere gratitude for the countless contributions their family has made to the prosperity of our island."

With a subtle nod of shared understanding, the brothers raised their champagne glasses, embodying the grace and poise expected of their lineage.

The announcer continued, warmly addressing the crowd, "And now, it is my pleasure to introduce our Prime Minister, who will share his greetings and insights with us."

The prime minister approached the podium, his sharp black suit, glasses, neatly cut hair, and noticeable nose commanded attention.

Miguel, seemingly unimpressed, inspected his glass before glancing up, his expression one of surprise.

"Wait, he's still the prime minister? I swear, they need to start electing younger folks," he muttered.

Bianca and Malachi shot Miguel a warning look, and Bianca whispered through gritted teeth, "Shut up."

Meanwhile, the prime minister engaged the crowd with a jovial tone, "How's everybody doing? I see you all dressed nicely," eliciting laughter from the audience.

Getting to the heart of his speech, the Prime Minister declared, "We stand at a historic juncture. We have liberated ourselves and emerged as a sovereign nation." The crowd erupted into enthusiastic applause.

"With this new chapter, we move forward without the shadow of colonial rule—who needs to say more?" he continued, his voice filled with conviction. "In just 30 days, our clans will convene to forge crucial alliances with the clans of the Emerald Isles, a bold step toward strengthening our collective prosperity and affirming Jamaica's place as a leading force in the region."

Malachi, ever unreserved in sharing his perspective, interjected, "I'm not sure this is the best course of action."

He continued, "Rushing into alliances without a comprehensive understanding of the landscape could lead to unforeseen consequences. Our country is facing challenges, and the people require genuine support, not mere political posturing."

With that, he took a measured sip of his drink, as if to steady himself after conveying the gravity of his concerns.

Deon, dressed in a sharp green suit with his arms casually out of the jacket, jumped into the conversation with a playful grin.

"What's your alternative, Malachi? Just sit back and watch?"

His locs were tied in a bun, the sides of his head shaved, while a few strands framed his face, adorned with gold clips at the ends.

"You think it's a bad idea, huh?" Deon teased. "Consider the possibilities—forming alliances could provide the strategic advantage we've been lacking.

We'd gain access to new resources and increased support... or are you simply resistant to change?"

He relished the moment, eager to challenge Malachi's perspective.

Malachi set his glass down with a deliberate motion, fixing Deon with a steely gaze. "Come on now," he replied, sarcasm lacing his tone.

"It's not about fear; it's about pragmatism. The Prime Minister seems more intent on consolidating power while the most vulnerable among us are struggling to get by."

Attitudes like yours only push away those who could help us."

His words were sharper than intended, and the room fell silent, the weight of his truth hanging in the air.
He'd sell us out if it meant lining his pockets."

He nodded towards the podium where promises flowed freely.

"Change is needed, but not the nonsense these so-called leaders offer."

Malachi paused the weight of his grandfather's legacy clear in his stance.

"We're not here just to uphold old reputations.

This is our time to lead, to be the change our elders hoped for."

His words hung in the air, leaving Deon silent and the room reflective, aware that new leaders were stepping onto the scene.

Bianca's jaw clenched, a smile blooming on her face.

Her head bobbed, a nervous tic.

Miguel clapped Malachi on the back, his hand heavy.

"Albert Einstein himself couldn't have said it better!"

The music started, a lively beat filling the ballroom.

Bianca, noticing the group of elite guests observing Malachi from behind, subtly moved closer.

A woman in a teal dress approached their table, her smile bright. She lightly touched Malachi's arm, her touch lingering just a moment longer than necessary. "Malachi," she murmured, her voice a low, melodious hum, "such a shame to let this beautiful music go to waste.

The dance floor's just over there."Miguel's eyebrows shot up in surprise. Malachi, initially hesitant, began, "Nah, I'm—"

Before he could finish, Miguel faked a cough, his hand briefly disappearing inside his collar. "Negro, if you ever…" he said, a smirk on his face, clearly relishing the banter.

Malachi gave Miguel a look of bewildered annoyance, mouthing, "What the heck are you doing?" He then changed his mind, a smile spreading across his face.

 "On second thought," he said seizing the opportunity, grasped Bianca's hand and pulled her onto the dance floor.

On the dance floor, as the soft music enveloped them, she wrapped her arms around his neck with a tender familiarity.

He swallowed nervously, his bottom lip folding under his teeth, a small "hmph" escaping as he tried to contain his uncertainty. They were eye to eye, her smile warm and inviting.

"What?" he managed to ask, trying to mirror her ease.

"What do you mean, what?" she teased gently. "Would you rather I just not make eye contact?"

He glanced away for a moment, a bashful smile tugging at his lips.

"No, no," Malachi replied quickly, his gaze catching sight of a man in a sharp black-and-white suit dancing with a girl.

The man had short, curly hair, a black jacket over a white turtleneck, and red-tinted shades perched on his nose.

He moved with easy confidence, already circling with another woman as he nodded curtly to Malachi.

Malachi nodded back before returning his gaze to her.

"Mal, are you okay?" she asked, concern underlying her gentle tone.

"Yeah, I am," he replied, though the words felt thin.

"Seriously, Malachi, are you alright?" she asked, her concern genuine.

"I'm good. Are you good?" he deflected lightly, his hands briefly resting on her shoulders, the scent of her perfume—something floral and subtly spicy—washing over him.

"Don't turn this back on me," she replied gently, her tone both understanding and firm.

"I asked because I know loss all too well. As a former foster child, I understand your pain after losing your father."

He spun Bianca around gracefully, the world blurring past in a whirl of colors.

Yet, as he twirled her, Malachi's thoughts drifted to his father. Each turn felt like a reminder of the weight of expectations pressing down on him, the burden of living up to his father's legacy.

Beneath the vibrant facade, grief swirled within him, a shadow that darkened the joy of the moment, making each spin feel bittersweet.

He forced a smile, but the ache in his chest lingered, a silent testament to the loss he carried.

"Honestly, I'm a complete mess," he confessed, his voice trembling with vulnerability as the weight of his emotions poured out.

"Not only that, everyone expects me to be just like him. And I look just like him."

As he spun Bianca around, a surge of conflicting emotions washed over Malachi—admiration intertwined with grief, and a profound longing for the father he had lost.

Each twirl felt like a dance with memories, the laughter of the moment clashing with the weight of expectation.

The joy of the dance was tinged with heartache, as he grappled with the impossibility of living up to a legacy while yearning for the warmth of his father's presence.

As Bianca's words of encouragement pierced through the storm of doubt clouding Malachi's mind, her eyes softened, offering a beacon of light in his moment of vulnerability.

"Mal," she whispered, her voice thick with unshed tears and a yearning that ached deep within her, "you can be your own man.

Forge your path—not just as a Shaka or your father's son. Let them see you for who you truly are.

Be the man God intends you to be. Please, let me see you."

Her hand reached out, trembling slightly as if she dared to hope he might finally embrace the freedom she so desperately wanted for him.

Her words resonated deeply within him, a stark contrast to the flashbacks that haunted him.

Memories of family members urging him to follow in his father's footsteps, coupled with the harsh training regimens orchestrated by his uncle to push his limits in harnessing the family's lunar abilities, flooded his mind.

The weight of expectations and the pressure to emulate his father's legacy bore down on him, but in Bianca's words, he found a glimmer of hope and a chance to forge his path.

Those words found a place in his heart, and he held onto them fiercely.

She nestled her head against his chest, the steady rhythm of his heartbeat resonating like a soothing melody.

With a gentle sigh, she closed her eyes, letting the warmth of the moment envelop her.

"Do that," she whispered, her voice barely a breath, "and that's the man I want to see. The one who knows his worth and isn't afraid to reveal it." She pulled back slightly, searching his eyes, ready to lay her heart bare. "Because that's the man I've been hoping you'd become."

He felt a flicker of warmth at her reassurance. "Oh, so you do like me," he teased, a hint of newfound confidence shining through his voice.

She looked up at him, her eyes sparkling with amusement, but then her gaze drifted to the massive window, the light filtering in and casting a soft glow around them.

A blurry figure moved outside the glass, drawing her attention.

"What was that?" she asked, a flicker of alarm threading through her voice.

His heart raced at the sudden shift in her demeanor. He followed her gaze, anxiety prickling at the back of his mind. Just as he opened his mouth to respond, a deafening explosion shattered the stillness of the room.

The wall burst apart like fragile glass, debris flying through the air with terrifying force. Pain erupted in his head as something struck him, and in an instant, the world faded to black.

To be continued...

CHAPTER 10- SOIREE INCIDENT

The ballroom was a charnel house. A gaping maw in the wall, a testament to some colossal force, spewed debris across the polished marble floor, amongst which lay lifeless.

Panic reigned. People scrambled for cover behind overturned tables and heavy drapes, their terror palpable in the desperate silence between screams.

But above the human fear, a far more chilling horror moved.

Grotesque serpentine creatures, their forms hunched and brutal, swarmed the fallen, their vile task the methodical draining of life force.

Their feeding was a macabre ballet, each movement a sickening whisper of dread.

High on the balcony, Malachi awoke with a jolt.

The distant screams, the shattering destruction below, ripped him from unconsciousness. A sharp pain in his side anchored him to the brutal reality.

Bianca and Noah, the curly-haired young man, stood at the balcony's golden railing, their whispers urgent against the chaos below.

"They're everywhere," Noah muttered, his eyes darting nervously across the scene, scanning for any signs of danger.

Bianca nodded, her expression tense. "All I see are shadows," she said, her voice barely above a whisper.

Behind Malachi, an elderly couple huddled, their fear silent but profound. Beside them, a mother clutched her young son, her protectiveness a desperate shield.

Bianca spotted Malachi stirring. Relief flooded her features. She rushed to him, pulling him into a fierce hug.

"Hey," Malachi said, surprised. "What's going on?"

Bianca pulled back, her eyes searching his. "I thought you were dead," she breathed, her voice thick with emotion.

He stood, his gaze catching on the curly-haired guy, a face he recognized from the dance floor before the... *explosion*. They exchanged a fleeting, knowing nod.

"It's a bloodbath down there," Bianca whispered, her voice trembling with urgency.

She pulled him to the railing.

"Some lizard-looking things," Noah added, his voice flat. "Attacked out of nowhere."

Bianca gestured towards Noah. "Malachi, this is Noah. He saved you."

Malachi nodded, a flicker of gratitude. "Thanks, man." Noah offered a modest smile.

An older man nearby shook his head, his confusion clear. "What are you talking about?

It's like trying to make sense of a storm from behind a closed door."

Malachi ran a hand through his hair. What kind of chaos had he stumbled into?

Engulfed by explosions, screams, and monster roars, he glanced at Bianca and exclaimed, "Weren't we just at a soirée? Since when did we jump planets?"

Bianca's gaze sharpened. She pointed towards the source of the guttural sounds. "Go take a look."

He felt it then—a discordant hum, resonating not just in his ears but deep within his bones.

A subtle tremor of Spiritual Energy, a ripple of cosmic imbalance, like the faint aftershock of a universal earthquake.

A cold, weightless pressure, a profound sense of wrongness that spoke to his innate understanding of cosmic justice.

But interwoven with that subtle tremor was something far more visceral—pure, unadulterated evil.

A searing heat, a stench of decay and malice that clawed at his mind.

This was not a subtle pressure; it was the raw, untamed energy of chaos, intent on obliteration.

He descended, each step bringing him closer to the heart of the turmoil.

Bodies lay strewn across the marble, limbs twisted at unnatural angles.

A horde of serpentine creatures dominated the scene. Their bodies were a mottled green and grey, segmented like colossal snakes yet possessing hulking humanoid torsos and arms. Sharp, red-tipped spines jutted from their backs and shoulders.

Their reptilian faces, with glowing yellow eyes, burned with predatory intensity.

Their mouths were filled with needle-sharp teeth. Dark, almost black, armored plating covered parts of their bodies, contrasting with the smoother texture of their limbs and tails.

Those powerful tails were wrapped around the corpses of several powered individuals.

The pattern of death was horrifyingly consistent. Each victim's mouth was agape, a faint blue light clinging to their lips – a chilling testament to their life force being cruelly drained.

The creatures had used their tails to restrain their victims, forcing their mouths open before absorbing the blue energy into their gaping maws.

The brutality solidified Malachi's decision to remain hidden, to observe.

His eyes widened in horror at the chaos unfolding below.

Three figures fought fiercely against the horde.

Amidst the swirling chaos, a man in a tattered purple suit, with braids tied into a topknot and eyes glowing a fierce violet, engaged in a fierce struggle with a serpentine creature.

His movements were a symphony of desperate precision. Vivid red markings flickered across his chest beneath his clothing, throbbing with an otherworldly energy.

With a forceful blow, he sent the creature crashing to the ground, then relentlessly continued his assault, each strike echoing with power.

Around him, people dashed frantically, their hurried steps a backdrop to his determined onslaught.

Then, a figure cut through the creatures like a scythe. His nappy hair barely stirred as he moved with impossible speed, his yellow eyes blazing, unleashing searing beams of light.

Each blast erupted in a spray of thick, black blood as the creatures convulsed and fell.

Twin laser blasts erupted from his eyes, obliterating a section of the horde. Another, in a blue suit, launched into the air, unleashing rapid, controlled blasts.

Though seemingly new to their powers, their fighting improved, hinting at a potential to hold their own.

As Malachi turned back to the group on the balcony, the old man studied him for a moment and then nodded slowly. "You're Enoch's son, aren't you?" he said, a hint of curiosity in his voice.

Bianca quickly cut him off. "Not now, sir," she said, her tone soft but firm. She looked at Malachi. "Are you okay?"

Malachi sighed. "Look, I can't stick around for this," he said, turning to leave.

Bianca grabbed his hand. He paused, surprised. She released him quickly, her face flushed. Noah raised an eyebrow.

Bianca's voice took on an urgent tone. "Malachi, you can't just bail.

We've been waiting for you to wake up. With Miguel and Deon gone, you're the best shot we have if we want to get out of here."

Malachi let out a sarcastic chuckle. "Oh sure, so now I'm the one who's supposed to save the world?"

Bianca leaned closer, her eyes fixed on him. "Isn't your family the guardian clan? You're supposed to be the protector."

Their argument heated up. Malachi insisted he wanted to leave, but Bianca wasn't backing down. She sighed deeply. "What happened to want to make your path? Where's that fire?"

Malachi felt the familiar push from his family, the pressure to be a leader like his father hanging over him. It was a struggle that scrambled his thoughts and weighed on his heart.

Unwilling to show any weakness, he masked his turmoil with a brave face.

"Fine, I'll do it," he said, forcing enthusiasm despite the internal battle.

Noah stepped in. "I got your back, man," he said, his eyes serious.

The old man chuckled condescendingly, shaking his head. "Oh, the things you youngsters believe these days... It's like you've lost all sense of reality.

The world isn't changing; it's just the same old nonsense in flashy new clothes.

"Malachi shook his head, irritated by the casual dismissal. He then realized something – Bianca was half-awakened. He would keep that to himself for now.

He turned to Noah. "Let's go."

He turned to Bianca, handing her his phone. "B, stay here and try to call my family," he instructed, his gaze lingering on her. "Here's my password."

Bianca took the phone, worry etched on her face. "Why not call the JDF?"

"They would've been here by now if it were that simple," he said, his voice tinged with urgency. "I think something bigger's going on."
He took a deep breath and leaped over the balcony railing, channeling his Spiritual Energy.

The sensation was electric, a surge of power igniting his senses.

  He landed with a thunderous impact, cracking the ground beneath him.

The monsters roared in response, their fury palpable. Just then, Noah landed beside him, unwavering and ready for the fight. "Watch out!" Noah yelled as a monster lunged.

Before it could reach Malachi, a man in a shredded purple suit appeared, delivering a bone-jarring blow that sent the creature reeling.

"Damn, you guys are still alive!" he exclaimed.

Malachi stared at the guy, feeling the air thrum with a vibrant energy that roared from within, filling the space with an intense presence.

The other two fighters were blasting their way through the horde. "Yo, they just keep coming!" Noah yelled.

Malachi shouted, "Focus on saving the people!"

The braided-haired guy turned to him. "What about you?"

Malachi's right hand vibrated with energy as a blade of electric blue light materialized, arcing from his fist.

The sword shimmered like liquid lightning, its swirling patterns pulsing with radiance. The guard formed a striking cross, symbolizing power and balance, while the blade flickered, casting a dazzling glow in the darkness.

A grin spread across Malachi's face as he began to back away.

"Me? I'm just going to play my part."

To be continued...

CHAPTER 11- SOIREE INCIDENT PT.2

Malachi assessed the chaotic battlefield, his mind racing. *Why tonight of all nights?* The weight of the situation pressed heavily on his chest, the acrid scent of smoke and sweat filling the air.

He turned, spotting the duo unleashing their powers, flashes of light and bursts of energy crackling around him. While others screamed in terror, desperately trying to escape.

In the chaos, he saw the guy man with the mini Afro, trapped in the clutches of a monstrous creature, its grip tightening like a vice.

With a determined grunt, Malachi shot forward, a blue streak blurring through the air. The world became a whirlwind of colors, the wind howling past him.

Adrenaline surged, sharpening his senses as he weaved through obstacles, closing in on the struggle ahead with razor-sharp focus.

In one swift motion, Malachi cleaved the creature in half, black, viscous blood splattering across the ground, a putrid scent rising as it howled in agony. Just then, a man's scream pierced the air. Without hesitation, Malachi dashed up the stairs, his heart racing.

He spotted the creature looming over the man, monstrous and menacing. With fierce determination, Malachi charged forward, using his sheer strength to grapple with the beast. He wrestled it away from the man.

Malachi reached for the man, grabbing his arm, but he was struck by the shock of how frail the guy was—skinny to the bone, his skin clammy and pale, eyes hollow and vacant, reflecting a haunting despair.

As he pulled, the man's arm tore off in Malachi's hand, the sickening sound of flesh ripping filling the air. Stunned, Malachi stared at the severed limb, the warmth of blood coating his palm.

"Damn it!" he exclaimed, the weight of the moment crashing down on him, a mixture of fury and helplessness surging within.

Malachi looked up just as a massive tail slammed into him, sending him sprawling into the ballroom.

He collided with a pillar, shattering stones and sending debris flying. Dazed, he lay amidst the chaos, acutely aware that his sword had vanished, highlighting the peril of his predicament.

As Malachi lay against the shattered pillar, he muttered, "I didn't sign up for this."

Panic flickered in his mind as he wondered, **where is Miguel?** Just then, he realized he was surrounded by the creatures, their menacing forms closing in, cutting off any chance of escape.

Suddenly, the creatures stopped fighting and focused solely on him. Noah shouted, "No! They're going after Malachi!"

As the fearsome creatures circled Malachi, a bolt of yellow lightning split the sky, striking two of them down. Malachi caught sight of Noah, standing with his palms outstretched and still smoking from the discharge.

Noah nodded, a quick confirmation of his role in the sudden turn of events. "Alright," Malachi murmured, springing into action.

With a swift motion, he formed his sword, its blade glinting ominously. He launched into a whirlwind of movement, blitzing through the chaos with relentless precision.

In just thirteen minutes, he had dispatched the creatures, leaving the battlefield eerily silent in the wake of his deadly efficiency. Revitalized, Malachi moved with a fierce, unyielding energy. He darted through the fray, each movement a blend of speed and precision, striking down foes with unmatched agility and strength.

The defeated creatures began to disintegrate, their forms dissolving into ashes that spiraled upward like specters finally at peace.
The men stood in awe at what they had witnessed. One murmured, "Remind me never to piss him off," prompting laughter from the group as they broke the tension of the moment.

The braided-haired guy broke the silence, his voice shaky. "Okay, what was that?"

At that moment, transparent blue orbs began to rise and float through the walls, casting a soft glow across the battlefield.

Everyone paused, captivated by the ethereal sight.

The orbs danced gracefully, illuminating their expressions of awe and confusion, as they waited for what would happen next in this surreal encounter.

The guy, with the braids, watched in disbelief, whispering, "Is this real?" as he crossed himself.

The man in the blue suit, usually unflappable, loosened his tie and muttered, "I've seen some things, but nothing like this."

Noah, regaining his senses, was frozen in awe. "How... do you explain this?" he wondered aloud, his voice tinged with fear and wonder.

The room remained hushed, filled only with the soft rustle of spirits ascending, leaving the group bound in shared awe at the extraordinary sight.

Malachi, still huffing from the battle, raised his gaze to the shimmering forms ascending through the air.

Narrowing his eyes, he tried to pierce the mystery of what he was witnessing.

What on earth are these? he pondered, his mind grappling with the reality of the souls drifting beyond.

The scene unfolded like a dream—otherworldly and profoundly unsettling—casting a shadow over the night's already incredulous events.

As Noah spoke, two guys walked up to him—one sporting braids, the other in a white shirt.

"What's up, yo!" the guy in the braids called as he approached Noah, giving a quick hand clap before pulling Noah in for a one-armed hug.

"I'm Jermaine!" He then stepped back and gestured toward Fabian. "This is my homeboy, Fabian."

Noah said, giving them fist bumps. "What a night, huh?"

Jermaine nodded, a grin spreading across his face. "Tell me about it."

Malachi, within earshot, listened in, curious about their introductions.

Impressed by their skills, Noah said, "You guys were doing your thing out there! What powers do you have?".

Jermaine nodded, a confident grin spreading across his face. "Yeah, I'm pretty strong, and my body feels tougher than usual. It's kinda wild."

His eyes momentarily blazed a glowing yellow before reverting to their usual deep black.

"Well, at least my senses are better," he said with a hint of a wry smile, "so I ain't mad at it."

Suddenly, as if it were his turn to speak, Fabian jumped in with animated gestures. "I just realized I can grab energy, soak it up, and use it. It's wild, and I'm still figuring it out!"

The guy in the singed blue suit approached his distinct features a harmonious blend of African and Chinese descent.

Noah glanced to the side, doing a double-take at the guy in the blue suit. "Ronaldo, is that you?" he finally said. The guy turned to look at him, and Noah wiped the corners of his lips in disbelief. "Holy crap, it's you! It's me, Noah. We used to go to the same primary school."

Ronaldo clicked his tongue in recognition. "Oh, Noah Power, what's good, man?" They pulled each other into a one-arm hug, and Noah patted his back, laughing.

As they separated, Ronaldo grinned and said, "Of course, you were the fastest kid in our club! How you've been, though?"
Noah chuckled, replying, "I've seen better days, bro."

Jermaine, curious, chimed in, "So, Ronaldo, what powers you got?"

Ronaldo flexed his fingers, and an orb of fiery energy crackled to life in his palm, shimmering with intensity before it diffused and vanished, leaving the group in stunned silence.

Ronaldo chuckled, a playful grin spreading across his face. "Man, I'm not entirely sure what it is, but whatever it does, it goes boom."

Jermaine leaned in, a hint of envy mixed with curiosity in his eyes. "Man, I'm the only one here without any cool powers."

Malachi approached the group, his expression betraying a hint of frustration.

"You've been awakened," he stated matter-of-factly. "It's nothing out of the ordinary these days - like half the world is going through this same thing."

He let that sink in before adding, "You've tapped into a deeper level of awareness. Those abilities you're noticing? They're part of this change."

The easygoing way they handled the news surprised him. Malachi still disliked being thrust into the role of mentor, but here he was, once again, guiding them through the unexpected.

Malachi sighed, a hint of frustration in his voice. "I know this is overwhelming. You're not alone—this awakening is happening to many people."

"You've reached a higher state of consciousness, with all its responsibilities," he continued, pausing to push his locs out of his face.

Fabian chimed in, "What causes it?"

Malachi met his gaze, his voice steady. "The near-death experience you just went through. That's often what triggers it."

Jermaine perked up and asked, "Wait, do you mean a spiritual awakening?"

Noah chuckled, "Yup, that's one way to put it."

Jermaine's face lit up. "Man, I've been on my spiritual journey for a while now.

"I was once a soccer player," he began, his voice tinged with nostalgia. "But an injury changed everything. After losing my brother, I sought solace in St. Catherine, where I ultimately found God."

Now, all this is happening!"

The guys around him nodded, understanding his struggles. Noah and Fabian offered their sympathy, and Malachi, though itching to leave, realized he had to step up and take some responsibility, even though he wasn't thrilled about it.

Ronaldo took a deep breath, trying to maintain focus. "Alright, we've got powers now, which is cool. But what I want to know is why those lizard things were after us and what the heck they are."

Noah nodded in agreement. "You're right. I think they wanted our powers, but once they spotted Malachi, they all turned on him."

Everyone turned their glares toward Malachi.

Malachi glanced around at them, meeting their stares with a calm demeanor. "What?" he said, raising an eyebrow, clearly unfazed by their scrutiny.

Suddenly, a girl crashed through the ballroom's glass doors, tripping over bodies scattered in her way.

"Somebody help, me!" she shouted, her voice filled with panic.

She glanced back just in time to see two creatures burst through the doors, shattering them into pieces. She screamed and fell to the floor, terror evident in her eyes.

In a sudden burst of motion, Malachi vanished, leaving behind a luminous streak of blue that rippled like a wave through the air.

A gust of wind tousled the group as Noah approached, his face lit up with an infectious grin.

"Did you guys see that?" he exclaimed, laughter bubbling up and escaping through his partly covered mouth, eyes wide with astonished disbelief.

Meanwhile, Malachi swiftly scooped up the girl. Ronaldo vanished with a series of crackling pops, reappearing in front of the creatures.

 He extended his hands, unleashing small explosions from his palms that obliterated them. Simultaneously, Malachi flickered away, the girl secured in his arms.

Malachi landed gracefully on the staircase with the girl in tow, glancing up to where Bianca and the others were.

The young woman sat trembling with fear, tears streaming down her face, unable to hide her terror.

Her dark skin and unraveled braids told of her struggles, as did the blood-smeared black dress.

Tear-streaked makeup evidenced her distress, while her shining lip gloss highlighted the contrast of her striking gray eyes.

Malachi, with gentle calmness, assured her, "It's alright, you're safe now," feeling deep sympathy for her plight.
He sensed a powerful shift in the air, as her Spiritual Energy spiked, mirroring her emotional turmoil.

As the group gathered, Jermaine asked quietly, "What happened?" Fighting to speak through her shock, she replied, "Those things... they killed my sister right in front of me. I... I..." Her voice broke with grief.

Noah interjected, firm yet comforting, "Hey, everything's going to be alright. We'll get you out of here," offering a promise of safety and hope.

Malachi felt the energy around her intensify, each pulse echoing her profound sorrow and fear.

Malachi watched as Alexis's eyes shifted, turning white with a sharp slit down the middle. Confused, she asked, "What's happening?" The guys instinctively stepped back, and Fabian muttered, "She got powers too?"

Alexis waved her hands animatedly, trying to express what she felt inside. "There's this thing," she struggled, almost as if she could touch it. "It's like... right there, but I can't quite get hold of it."

She looked at the others with wide eyes, her voice tinged with panic. "I'm hearing everything, guys—the wind, cars, even your breathing. It's overwhelming, like a war zone in my head!"

In her rising panic, she clutched her head and shouted, "I can't take it anymore!" Her voice exploded outward in a sonic blast, sending ripples through the air.

Malachi's eyes widened in alarm. "Run!" he shouted to the guys, urgency lacing his tone.
Her scream cut through the air with brutal ferocity, causing the room to tremble around them. In quick response, Malachi raised his arms, summoning a shimmering barrier to shield them from the onslaught.

The impact created ripples across the barrier, making the very walls shudder as dust vibrated in the chaotic energy. Overhead, light bulbs shattered, raining down a cascade of glass.

The men stood behind Malachi, hands pressed against their ears, groaning as a trickle of blood marked the violence of the assault on their senses.

As the overwhelming noise subsided into an uneasy silence, the room was filled only with the sound of strained walls creaking.

Alexis looked around at everyone, her eyes wide with concern. "I'm so sorry, guys! I didn't mean to do that!"

Fabian said, "Nah, you're good. Just warn us next time, alright?" He chuckled, and the girl replied with a smile, "Okay!"

He chuckled a nervous sound that didn't quite reach his eyes. Malachi glanced at Alexis, concern etched on his face. "You alright?" he asked softly.

Meanwhile, Jermaine was complaining about his ears, covering them repeatedly. "Man, that was way too loud!"

Fabian rolled his eyes and replied, "Man, You'll live."

Jermaine suddenly paused, sniffing the air. "Hold up," he said, alert. Malachi looked over, listening intently. "You guys hear that?" Noah asked her. "What is it?"

Just as Malachi caught the faint sound of approaching footsteps, the side wall blasted inward, debris flying and chaos erupting once more. Instinctively, they all flinched, with Fabian shielding her as she screamed amidst the unfolding turmoil.

A man flew backward into the room, tumbling and crashing into a pile of rubble.

Right behind him, Miguel and Deon rushed in. Deon's locs hung in his face, giving him a wild look, and his left sleeve was ripped, showing some skin.

Miguel wasn't wearing much, just white pants, but glowing fire markings covered his upper body, and his arms radiated a fiery orange light. His locs and eyes blazed with the same intense heat.

The man was a mess—burnt, slashed, clearly injured. He was on one knee, clutching at his hip, black blood welling between his fingers.

Despite the horrific wounds, a chilling laugh erupted from him.

He rose, his movements surprisingly fluid despite his condition, and his gaze fell upon Malachi.

His eyes, glowing with an unnatural, crimson light—like the eyes of a goat—fixed on Malachi, who instinctively ushered Alexis behind him.

The other guys, Fabian, Jermaine, Ronaldo, and Noah, automatically flanked Malachi, forming a protective circle.

Malachi's eyes widened in recognition as he realized the man was the valet from earlier. Disbelief crossed his face, and he narrowed his gaze, recalling the valet's flirtation with Bianca. His expression hardened.

The red, goat-like eyes, the black blood—it wasn't human. It was something else entirely, something far more dangerous than he had anticipated.

To be continued

CHAPTER 12- SOIREE INCIDENT PT.3

Miguel stepped forward, urgency in his voice. "Malachi, that valet is responsible for everything. He's the one pulling the strings."

Fabian's eyes glowed intensely, radiating an otherworldly brilliance. His arms shimmered with glowing white light, swirling patterns of energy dancing along their length, illuminating the opulent foyer.

Jermaine's muscles bulged, tearing his clothes as red lines emerged beneath his shirt, tracing fierce patterns across his chest.

The valet stood with his arms extended wide, wounds visibly healing before their eyes. A smirk spread across his face as he admitted, "It's me. So What are you gonna do about it?"

The valet stood tall, a cruel smirk on his face as the wound on his hip healed, along with all his other injuries.

Deon sucked his teeth, annoyance etched on his face.

 In Deon's hand, the arrow materialized with an ethereal glow, capturing the silvery hues of the night. As he hurled it forward, casting radiant light across the shadows, he commanded, "Man, stop your noise."

The valet deftly sidestepped the incoming arrow, his eyes tracking its trajectory as it streaked past him with blinding speed. It struck a distant pillar, erupting into a dazzling burst of light and energy.

The valet glanced at the destruction, then at Deon. "You trying to kill me, bro?" he said, still in shock.

Suddenly, Miguel appeared in a flash, flames blasting from his feet. His knee smashed into the valet's face, sending a spray of blood through the air before the valet's body crumpled to the ground.

Struggling to regain his senses, the valet blinked rapidly, the fight momentarily knocked out of him as he lay amidst the debris, astonished by the sheer force of the strike.

Malachi watched, the scene unfolding before him. "Alright, guys, how about you guys get out of here," he ordered.

Jermaine shook his head. "Nah, I ain't going nowhere."

Noah gave Malachi a reassuring pat on the shoulder. "Remember, I told you I got your back."

Ronaldo, fidgeting, muttered, "I don't know what's up with you guys, but I'm out of here."

Before he could take another step, Alexis declared, "I'm coming with you." Ronaldo, surprised but relieved, simply nodded, "Alright, come on then ."

Hugging Malachi, she whispered, "Thanks for saving me." He smirked, amused at how he almost bailed.

"Come out of this alive," she grinned, adding, "The world needs more guys like you." With that, she ran off with Ronaldo. Malachi chuckled, her words echoing in his mind and finding the entire situation unexpectedly amusing, a smile spreading across his face.

The chaos around him couldn't entirely diminish the warmth spreading through Malachi.

 He was struck by how much larger and more muscular Jermaine appeared.

Jermaine dashed towards the valet, moving so quickly he was little more than a blur slicing through the chaos.

Fabian, standing firm, thrust his palm forward; a white projectile shot swiftly from his hand, streaking over Jermaine's shoulder with a faint whistle.

The projectile struck the valet, searing through his shoulder with a sizzling crack, and he staggered back, clutching the burning wound.

"God damn," he muttered, a grimace twisting his blood-smeared lips.

The valet blinked in bewilderment, trying to focus through the pain, but before he could react further, the blur materialized beside him.

Jermaine appeared, eyes glowing purple, moving with a primal grace. His fist collided with the valet, sending him crashing to the ground.

The earth quaked beneath them, spiderweb cracks radiating from the impact.

The air was filled with the stench of dust and the echoing crack of earth splitting, causing Miguel and Deon to steady themselves.

Deon approached, a triumphant grin on his face, and patted Jermaine on the shoulder, murmuring, "My man."

The valet lay on his stomach, blood trickled from his lips onto the cracked concrete, each ragged breath causing his muscles to tense and his eyes to flicker in pain.

He leaned up, shaking his head with a resigned bitterness. "Damn," he rasped, his voice rough and pained. "You boys gonna kill me."

Deon twirled his hand, summoning a flash of moonlight that coalesced into a bolt hovering before him.

With a confident snap of his fingers, the bolt shot toward him, drawing the wide-eyed gaze of the valet.

Swiftly, the valet swiped his hand, conjuring a shadowy barrier to intercept the bolt. It smashed against the dark shield, erupting in a blinding flash of light.

In a blur of motion, Miguel appeared, driving his hands into the shadow to tear it apart as flames erupted, burning the remnants away.

Deon followed with precision, driving a celestial arrow into the valet's shoulder.

The force pulled him back, pinning him against the wall with such impact that the valet was lodged into it, blood seeping from the wound and trickling down the shattered surface.
The valet, overwhelmed with disbelief, looked at Deon. "What exactly are your powers?" he asked. "I know your family deals with moonlight, but this... this defies all reason."

Deon tilted his chin upward slightly, eyes fixed on the valet with an unsettling intensity as if he were considering a delicacy.

Miguel approached Deon with a somber expression, his features carved with concern.

Malachi then spotted Deon and shouted, "Yo!" Deon turned back, momentarily surprised.

Malachi asked, "What do you think you're doing?" With an exasperated sigh, Deon remarked, "Sometimes, I truly believe Malachi is blind."

Malachi shook his head, striving to maintain his composure.

Malachi, his hands moving animatedly as he spoke, conveyed an urgent plea.

"Think this through," Malachi urged. "What do we lose if we kill him now? What if he's part of something bigger?" His eyes searched his companions, seeking understanding amid the tension.

Miguel placed a steadying hand on Deon's shoulder. "Yeah He's right, D," he said calmly.

Deon sucked his teeth in frustration, the sound sharp and dismissive.

Without uttering another word, Deon turned on his heel and walked away, his departure laced with unspoken menace.

Watching him go, the valet muttered under his breath, "That kid's got some problems."

Deon shot him a cutting side-eye, a silent warning that held its weight.

Malachi smoothly stepped into the valet's line of sight, blocking any further exchange. His presence was commanding, yet calm.

The valet, wincing from the pain, looked up with a strained grin. "So, you boys gonna get this thing out of my shoulder or what?"

Both Malachi and Miguel leveled a piercing gaze at him, the intensity of their stare leaving little doubt about their intentions. The valet's grin faltered, and he quickly added, "No, okay, okay," as he realized negotiation was off the table.

"Now, I've got some questions for you," Malachi declared, his voice steady and unyielding. "And you're going to tell me what I want to know."

As he spoke, Malachi's seriousness deepened when he watched in disbelief as the valet's wounds and swollen face began to heal rapidly before his eyes.

The valet massaged his jaw and shoulder with surprising ease, prompting Malachi to wonder, who is this guy?

The valet's fingers danced nervously over his goatee, his eyes alight with a manic gleam.

"You want to know why?

Maybe it's because I tried saying what's up, and you just sidestepped me," he sneered, bitterness threading through his words.

Miguel shook his head. "Now that's petty."

The valet chuckled. "Nah, I'm playing. But honestly, I never believed in God."

Deon sucked his teeth in frustration. "Come on, man, we ain't got time to deal with your disbelief," he shot back, urgency clear in his voice.

"Well," the valet began, his voice edged with irritation, "as I was saying before I was rudely interrupted," he barked at Deon, eyes flashing.

He then turned back to Malachi, his tone shifting to an unsettling mix of reverence and disbelief.

"I never believed in God," he confessed, "not until I met His sons."

Malachi's curiosity piqued, he said, "You met the angels?" Internally, he couldn't help but reflect on how he had tried to live a righteous life and had never seen an angel.

Miguel asked skeptically, his eyes darting between Malachi and the valet, "You met an angel? As in, from heaven?"

The valet nodded. "Yeah, but one that's been cast out."

Deon scoffed, his voice tinged with doubt. "That's a lie... The gates of hell are sealed off, aren't they?"

A twisted grin crept onto his face as he chuckled darkly.

"Who told you that?" he sneered. "They've already told me the gates are wide open."

"You can thank those overseas scientists for that little oversight.

"Now the fallen ones—they're not just on a sightseeing tour.

They're hungry, and they're after souls. Your souls," he paused, his grin widening with malice, "well, the superhuman souls, to be exact."

To be continued...

CHAPTER 13 - SOIREE INCIDENT PT.4

Fabian and Jermaine moved alongside Noah, forming a steadfast line as they faced the valet.

The Valet's eyes sparkled with mischief, words dripping with mockery as he taunted Malachi, Deon, and Miguel, each taunt like a dagger intended to unsettle their resolve.

"I guess I'm talking too much.

With grim determination, the valet wrenched the arrow from his shoulder, brandishing it menacingly before him. He swung it wildly, forcing Malachi and Miguel to duck and weave, skillfully evading the sharp arcs as it sliced through the air.

Suddenly, Deon appeared in a blur, closing the distance in an instant. With relentless force, he drove his knee into the valet's chest, sending him crashing through the wall in an explosion of dust and debris.

"You guys good?" Deon asked, glancing at Malachi and Miguel.

Malachi wiped his nose, while Miguel managed a thumbs up amidst the chaos. Deon peered through the gaping hole that led into the theater room. "Crap, he's gone," Deon said, surprise evident in his voice.

"What?" Miguel asked, moving closer to see for himself. "Oh damn," he said, turning back to Deon, eyes wide with disbelief.

"Hold on, I'll see if I can find him," Malachi said, closing his eyes to focus. Searching was like trying to find a single whisper in a storm; he struggled to separate the chaotic energies around him.

He felt the familiar Spiritual pulses of Deon, Miguel, Fabian, and Jermaine, their auras flickering like beacons. But there was no trace of the valet as if he had vanished entirely.

Malachi's thoughts were cut short by sudden movement. The valet emerged from the dissipating smoke, moving with a predatory speed.

The scene was chaotic, with debris scattered around as if a storm had blown through. Before Malachi could react, the valet targeted Noah with a swift kick that sent him sprawling, the impact a jarring sound.

Deon scarcely registered the looming threat before a massive shadowy fist collided with his chest, sending him reeling backward, struggling to gasp for air.

Desperation driving him, Fabian unleashed a focused beam from his fingertips, but the valet slipped past the attack with agile precision.

The valet looked up as the trio turned toward him. "Crap," Miguel muttered. Deon summoned a dazzling staff, hurling it at the valet. It skimmed the valet's cheek, leaving a vivid line of blood.

The valet wiped the blood with a smirk. "Almost had me," he quipped, unfazed by the close call.

The valet taunted, "Which one of you wants to die first?" as shadowy claws emerged from his knuckles. Miguel assumed a fighting stance.

"Follow my lead," he instructed, his voice steady and resolved.

Suddenly, Deon became a blur of silver, his speed creating a sonic boom that reverberated around the room, stirring a fierce wind that forced the twins to shield their faces.

He slashed at the valet, only for him to dissolve into nothingness, like a shadow melting into the dim light.

A low whistle sliced through the air. Miguel turned with a noncommittal "Hmm?" Before he could react, a massive, shadowy hand – the size of a tractor wheel – slammed into his chest. The impact sent him sprawling, the breath knocked from his lungs. Blood blossomed across the cracked pavement where he landed.

The valet, a figure shrouded in darkness, said only, "Six."

With inhuman strength, the valet gripped Miguel, lifting him effortlessly as though he weighed nothing. Then, with a casual overhand throw, the valet hurled him through the plate-glass window, shattering it into a thousand glittering shards.

Malachi clenched his fist, and blue slits, like glowing fissures, opened along his forearms. An overwhelming rage consumed him, fueled by the searing memory of his twin brother bawling in his arms.

"You're going to die for that," Malachi growled, his voice thick with grief and fury. His eyes glowed with the same electric blue as the markings on his arms.

Brooks, startled, spun around. "What?" he stammered, his eyes widening.

Before Malachi could react, he swung his arm in a wild arc. A shadow, swift and silent as a dart, shot out from The valet, weaving through the air with unnatural speed. The shadow grazed Malachi's head, shearing off a couple of his dreadlocks.

A guttural growl ripped through the air. Malachi whirled, his breath catching in his throat as he saw Jermaine rising. Jermaine's fangs were bared in a snarl; his skin seemed to shimmer, and his eyes glowed with an intense, malevolent purple fire.

"Where's that black boy?" Jermaine demanded, his voice crackling with fury. "I'm going to kill that hombre."The valet's face twisted in shock, his bravado faltering for the first time.

The valet yelled, "Hombre, I'm right here!" His arms were spread wide.

Deon appeared beside Malachi, responding with a curt, "Alright, don't move." With a resonant thud, he jammed his staff into the ground, drawing a sharp glance from Malachi, whose eyes were filled with understanding and intent.

In the blink of an eye, Deon flashed behind the valet, seizing his hands with a swift, practiced motion. The valet's bravado shattered as he flicked his head in confusion. "What the—ahh!" he cried out in pain, surprise mingling with a grimace as Deon's grip tightened."Do your thing, bro," he urged Jermaine.

With a feral intensity, Jermaine began to slash at the valet's body, each swipe of his claws tearing flesh with visceral precision.

The valet's cries were muffled by the rhythmic swish of claws meeting flesh, the air thick with the coppery scent of blood, and the sight of dark gore splattering across the floor in a gruesome dance.

The valet's head, a grotesque parody of a human skull, bounced once, twice, along the foot of the staircase.

Jermaine stared, his eyes wide, his breath catching in his throat.

The detached gaze in his eyes was replaced by a dawning horror, the weight of his action settling upon him like a physical burden.

His face paled, the color draining from his lips as the reality of what he'd done crashed over him.

"Woah!" Deon exclaimed, his head bobbing rhythmically, a strange mix of awe and morbid fascination in his voice.

"That's how it's done!" His words hung in the air, jarringly out of sync with the grim scene.

Malachi watched, his mouth agape. The sheer stupidity of the situation washed over him.

These guys were unbelievably reckless. Malachi's usual moral compass spun wildly. *Seriously? Just like that?* He couldn't decide if he should intervene; his sense of right and wrong blurred.

The headless corpse, its momentum abruptly halted, stopped mid-fall. Deon stood staring at it, dumbfounded, his mind struggling to process the surreal sight before him.

A gruesome fountain of black, sulfur-smelling blood erupted from the severed neck, painting a macabre picture on the floor.

Then, as if by some perverse magic, the severed head was drawn back towards the body, the blood magically clotting and sealing the wound.

The flesh knitted itself back together, the head snapping back into place with a sickening *pop*. The eyes of the reanimated valet snapped open, focusing on Jermaine with pure, unadulterated malice.

Jermaine recoiled, his eyes bulging in disbelief. He stammered, unable to form coherent words.

The valet spun to face Deon just as a massive shadowy fist erupted through the rows of chairs, splintering wood and fabric alike. Malachi saw the threat unfolding and shouted, "No!" as he charged forward.

The valet, with a fluid motion, swung his arm, hurling a shadowy rod that pierced through the air and pinned Jermaine against the wall, high above the entrance of the ballroom.

Malachi skidded to a halt, momentarily frozen by the sight of blood trailing from Jermaine.

Alarmed, he glanced upward, just as a sphere of darkness hurtled toward him with unrelenting force.

The orb struck his abdomen with a searing burn, sending him skidding backward across the polished floor.

He tumbled between Noah and Fabian— Noah lay face down, unconscious and bleeding, while Fabian was sprawled on his back, the ground beneath him cracked from impact, his body marked by cuts and bruises.

The valet loomed over Malachi, a cruel smile playing on his lips. "Eeny, meany, miny, moe," he laughed, his voice dripping with malice. He pointed directly at Malachi.

"You," he declared with a sadistic glee, "I'm taking your soul first."Then, the sharp crack of a bullet sliced through the air, the valet's lower jaw shattering with visceral impact.

Bone splintered and teeth flew, the force of the shot snapping his head back violently.

Stunned, his body staggered, muscles reacting instinctively to the shock, struggling to remain upright.

Malachi turned his head sharply at the sound.

Malachi observed the new arrivals with unease. Dressed in green tactical gear and cloaks, their masked faces hidden beneath hoods, they moved with silent precision.

One of them lowered a smoking pistol, its barrel still warm from its recent shot.

At the forefront of this band stood an older man whose bearing was both commanding and composed.

A neatly trimmed grey beard added a dignified touch, while his eyes—one a striking blue, the other a rich brown—conveyed both wisdom and intensity.

His attire was a striking contrast to the menacing array around him.

Clad in a sophisticated teal suit, it spoke of elegance, yet strapped to his leg was a carbon steel sword, its presence a stark reminder of readiness for conflict.

When he spoke, his voice carried a weight that was impossible to ignore:

"Wolves, protect our people." It was more than a command; it was a rallying cry, a call to arms for the pack to shield their own against the encroaching chaos.

To be continued...

CHAPTER 14 - SOIREE INCIDENT PT.5

The bald man carefully walked through the chaos, his sharp eyes absorbing the grim scene—bones and clothing scattered everywhere, remnants of the fierce fight.

The machete at his hip rested securely in a sheath, its hilt protruding with an air of readiness.

The hilt was wrapped in worn leather, providing a reliable grip, and bore subtle notches that suggested years of use.

As the flickering lights swung overhead, the hilt caught the light, a silent reminder of the weapon's weight and its enduring purpose amidst the destruction.

He muttered, "What in God's name happened here?" while a few men tended to Deon's injuries. Meanwhile, others, weapons drawn, circled the valet, their movements tense and watchful.

He stopped in front of Malachi, a smirk playing on his lips. "Letting this dude get the drop on you, Malachi?" he taunted, exchanging a quick fist bump with him and Noah. "I thought I taught you to fight better than that."

Fabian came forward, supporting Jermaine, whose chest had a steaming hole that was slowly healing, though not completely closed.

The bald man arched an eyebrow in surprise. "You're a tough one, huh? You alive, son?"

With a weary but confident smile, Jermaine nodded. "Yeah, I'll live." Nearby, an agent led Deon away while the rest surrounded the valet, their weapons trained relentlessly on him.

"Uncle Vance, what's going on?" Malachi inquired his tone a mix of familiarity and urgency.

A shadow crossed Vance's face as he hesitated. "My apologies for the delay," he said, his voice low and controlled. "The island's in a full-blown crisis.

The clans are taking a brutal hit." He gestured towards the valet, the quiet menace in his demeanor unmistakable even in its restraint.
Malachi leaned in, his voice low and urgent. "Uncle, this guy's after our souls—and he's working with fallen angels."

Vance's eyes fixed on the valet, his expression hardening. The grim realization settled on his face.

"Seriously? Criminals and demons? Who knew that was a thing?" Vance muttered, a dark humor coloring his tone.

Miguel, his brow furrowed, asked, "You know him?"

Vance's eyes narrowed.

"That's Brooks," he stated flatly. "A name that should send shivers down the spines of every law enforcement officer on this island.

He's been a thorn in our side for years, and now this..." The unspoken threat hanging in the air was heavier than any weapon.

Jermaine, intrigued, tilted his head towards Vance, absorbing this new piece of information.

"Oh crap," Noah muttered, drawing the group's attention to the impossible sight before them.

They watched in disbelief as Brooks's shattered jaw began to mend itself, skin-like tentacles snaking out to fuse and form a perfect jawline.

Brooks chomped his restored jaw, shook his head, and yelled, "Woah!" his voice dripping with triumphant mockery.

Before anyone could react, an agent spoke urgently, "Awaiting your command, Inspector."

Brooks rose, exuding a confidence that teetered on arrogance. He called out, his voice smooth, laced with derision. "Inspector Vance! Always a pleasure. It feels like I've been waiting an eternity for your delightful company."

Unfazed, Vance clutched the hilt of his machete, his expression lined with weariness. "Brooks, these encounters are getting old.

How about we end this?" he suggested, his voice steady and resolute.

Brooks chuckled, the sound reminiscent of a snake's scales brushing against each other.

Brooks nodded, a menacing gleam in his eyes. "They certainly make an impression," he said with sardonic amusement.

Stepping closer, he added, "But tonight, the final curtain falls. Are you ready to leave this farce behind?" His words carried a chilling promise.

A shared glance passed between Vance, Malachi, and Noah. In a heartbeat, Vance's resolve sharpened. "Let's end this."

Gunfire shattered the night, bullets piercing the air.

A shadowy blanket enveloped Brooks as the gunfire ceased.

With a swift motion, he swiped his hand, dispelling the darkness and revealing his arm, now a smoky black.

"My turn," he intoned darkly.

With a decisive downward swipe, a streak of shadow lashed out, slicing through an agent with brutal precision.

The agent's body split apart, the halves falling to the ground in a gruesome display, the air heavy with the scent of blood and charred flesh.

The agent's eyes widened in stunned realization as Brooks flickered behind him.

The first agent, with metallic skin, charged, only to be crushed by shadowy tendrils. Two others attacked; one unleashed a bolt of electricity, and the other manipulated the marble floor. Brooks moved with lethal precision, snapping one adversary's neck effortlessly before turning to the next, tearing out their throat with ruthless efficiency.

An agent erected an energy barrier, but Brooks' shadow spear pierced it easily, leaving the agent lifeless.
One agent moved like a blur, but Brooks swiftly intercepted him, snapping his neck.

As a second agent stretched his limbs to entrap Brooks, and a third delivered baton blows, shadowy arms erupted *from within* tearing the stretchy agent apart in a gruesome spray.

He then dispatched the remaining agents with ruthless efficiency, reducing them to blood-soaked remains with precision and brutality.

Brooks surveyed the devastation with a twisted smile. "See how you've sent these gentlemen to their deaths," he taunted, pointing at Vance. "Shame on you." The shadows receded, leaving silence in the once-splendid ballroom.

Malachi placed a reassuring hand on his shoulder. "Uncle," he said, his voice low and steady, "just say the word.

With purpose, Vance turned to face his team—Malachi, Jermaine, Fabian, and Noah—his expression was a mix of authority and unyielding belief in his men.

Their eyes bore into him, seeking guidance amidst the storm.

"Listen, we're far from finished," Vance called out, his voice unwavering.

Brooks' gaze fell on Malachi, his cherished godsons. "You've been like sons to me, your strength and loyalty are my true anchors," he said, warmth threading through his voice.

Scanning the ravaged ballroom, he asked, "Where's Miguel?"

Noah, stepping through the debris, replied casually, "He got tossed outside."

Vance shrugged it off with a chuckle. "He'll live," he assured his tone light.

Turning to Jermaine, Fabian, and Noah, he said, "You earned my respect by standing and fighting alongside my boys when it mattered most."

He paused meaningfully. "But remember, courage means little if we don't survive this. This isn't our end; it's a test, and together we will see tomorrow."

Around them, the city descended further into chaos, echoing the fierce battle they faced. Malachi hesitated, glancing at Vance. "But, uncle —"

"No arguments!" Vance interjected. "This is it. I have to do this. You need to regroup and protect those who can't fight back right now."

Vance's hand rested on Malachi's shoulders, a moment of connection trying to push through the violence surrounding them.

The smile he managed was sincere, yet overshadowed by the weight of his decision—a smile Malachi recognized from their days of recovery.

"Once this is over, we'll be back on that field, playing like we always said we would. Now go—look after the others."

As Vance faced his destiny, Malachi lingered, his mind flooding with memories—days in the hospital where Vance's visits had become his anchor, solidifying their unspoken bond.

Noah nodded towards the door, his voice resolute. "You heard him. Let's go, man."

Malachi took a deep breath, bracing for what lay ahead. Vance was more than a leader in this battle; he was their beacon of courage and loyalty, inspiring them to believe in something greater.

Resolute, they turned away, prepared to fulfill their part in Vance's plan.

To be continued...

CHAPTER 15- SOIREE INCIDENT PT.6

The grand ballroom lay in ruins, its elegance marred by chaos. Shattered glass from the majestic chandeliers littered the floor, and tattered drapes fluttered in the night air.

Flickering sconces cast ghostly shadows, illuminating the valet as he deftly dispatched agents with chilling precision.

Amidst the destruction, Vance's unwavering gaze fixed on Brooks. In one smooth motion, he unsheathed a blade, its polished steel catching the faint light.

 Muscles coiled as his hand gripped the hilt firmly.

The high-tech alloy gleamed with an iridescent sheen, its flawlessly curved edge exuding precision. Intricate geometric patterns glowed faintly along the surface, suggestive of hidden technology.

"Brooks!" Vance's voice pierced the stillness, commanding attention. Brooks, momentarily shaken, released an agent to meet Vance's stare.

"This is your last mistake," Vance declared, his words heavy with finality.

Brooks chuckled, his confidence unshaken. "So, the mighty Vance shows his face. Took you long enough."

"You have no idea what you're up against," Vance warned.

Brooks shrugged casually. "I'm just getting mine. If taking down your clans is part of it, so be it."

Vance's eyes narrowed, his voice laced with a barely contained rage.

"You have no concept of the forces you're playing with, do you? The fallen angels you've allied yourself with will consume you, just as they'll consume everything in their path."

Brooks let out a barking laugh. "But you know what they say – if you can't beat 'em, join 'em."

Vance's jaw clenched, his knuckles turning white as he gripped the machete.

"You're a fool, Boy. Those creatures will use you and discard you without a second thought.

And if you think for one moment that I'm going to let you harm those children, you're sorely mistaken."

Brooks's eyes narrowed, and a flicker of uncertainty crossed his face. "Listen, Vance," he said grimly, "you better kill me right here. Because if I get out of this, I'm going after those kids."

Vance's expression turned serious as he held his blade, locking eyes with Brooks.

"Listen, Brooks," he said, calm but firm, "we've got big plans for those boys, and I'm ready to lay it all on the line to protect them.

So, if you want to test me, go ahead—try it."

Brooks tensed, his hands balling into fists. "Alright, Inspector, let's dance," he taunted. Vance slid into a sword stance, the gleaming blade held behind him, and replied with a smirk, "Let's."

In an instant, Vance zipped toward Brooks, leaving a trail of feathers in his wake.

Brooks, eyes wide with shock, leaned back just as Vance's blade nicked his throat. Clutching the slight cut, Brooks stepped back, muttering, "Really? The throat?"

With a hint of irritation, Vance replied, "Yeah, well, I've seen Endgame. You know how it goes—gotta aim for the head."

Brooks smirked, "That's why I like you, Inspector.

You're a no-BS kind of guy." With a casual flick of his finger, the air around him rippled violently, sending a visible wave of force barreling toward Vance.

But Vance, quick as lightning, blitzed behind Brooks, swinging his blade toward Brooks' neck.

Brooks grabbed the blade, a grunt escaping his lips as blood seeped between his fingers.

Vance slammed him to the ground, then swung him violently towards a wall.

Brooks landed, palms and feet splayed against the stone, a grin stretching across his face as he looked at Vance.

Vance gazed at Brooks, bewilderment etched into his features.

Brooks erupted into fits of wild laughter, eyes gleaming with a manic edge. "I thought you were the good guy," he sneered, his voice tinged with unsettling amusement and madness.

Vance locked eyes with Brooks, calm but sure. "So, you've finally lost it," he said.

Brooks chuckled darkly, "Lost what?"

Vance glanced at his machete and replied, "Well, as someone who fights for what's right, evil is always my enemy. And honestly, Brooks, you're kind of the embodiment of it.

"Brooks stood up, glancing at his now-healed palm with an unsettling grin.

"Funny, isn't it?" he said, brushing off dirt with a casualness that bordered on unnerving.

"You talk about honor all the time, but have you looked at what soldiers get up to?

That's not heroism, Vance, it's more twisted than that. And let's not kid ourselves here—you're not exactly squeaky clean, either."

His eyes flickered with a peculiar intensity, a hint of something unhinged lurking beneath the surface.

Vance shot Brooks a frustrated look. "You think you know everything, huh?"

He reached the collapsed staircase. Vance was gone. Brooks' face dropped. "What the hell?" he muttered,

 his eyes darting around the wreckage, a frantic energy replacing his previous calm.

"Where is he? Did he... did he escape?" He muttered to himself, his voice rising in pitch, searching every shadow, his gaze flitting from one impossible hiding place to another.

Suddenly, a flock of crows smashed into Brooks, driving him to the ground. The birds coalesced into the form of Vance, who swiftly pressed his machete against Brooks' throat.

The blade felt strangely cold against Brooks' skin. Vance's voice, usually calm, was strained, a tremor underlying his words.

"I'm concerned. What you've become... it's hurting me to even look at you.

This isn't you. This... darkness..." He paused, his grip tightening slightly on the blade but then relaxing again, the effort of holding himself back evident in the tremor of his hand.

"I can't kill you, Brooks. I can't. But I have to stop this. Despite the life you've chosen, I wanted to bring you over to the light.

But now, aligning with demons, I have no choice but to end this."

A faint, cruel smile stretched across Brooks' face. It was a smile devoid of warmth, twisted by delusion and something far more sinister.

"We already won, inspector," he whispered coldly, his eyes gleaming with chilling certainty, completely lacking any sense of the danger he was facing.

"This... power... it's intoxicating. It's mine.

You can't understand. The whispers, the visions... they're all real.

They tell me everything. They tell me I'm right.
And you... you're just another obstacle, another weakness to be overcome."

Brooks' body dissolved into a swirling mass of black smoke, silently reforming behind Vance with uncanny speed.

Before Vance could react, Brooks kicked his leg out from under him, forcing Vance to his knees.

With a firm grip, Brooks pulled Vance's head back, exposing his face to the shadows above.

Brooks hovered his free hand over Vance's face, and slowly, a mouth formed in his palm.

It opened wide, revealing rows of sharp, gleaming fangs. As if compelled by an unseen force, Vance's mouth opened in response.

From deep within him, a brilliant blue light began to flow, streaming from his mouth towards the hunger of the fanged maw in Brooks' palm.

The room was illuminated by the eerie glow as the light was steadily siphoned away, drawn into the dark depths of Brooks' hand, leaving Vance weakened and drained where he kneeled.

His skin lost its color, his eyes glazed over; each vanishing droplet stole his light, his life.

Brooks shoved Vance's body roughly to the ground, shaking his hand in disgust. "This is disgusting," he murmured, glancing down at Vance.

Brooks' gaze turned thoughtful as he addressed the fallen inspector. "Maybe you were a hero, the closest thing this country had to one, but I'm a devil now," he declared.

"I don't want to be saved. You had your way of life, and I have mine."

"I know how this looks, but I'm doing this for our people, for the island. Watch from above as I change the world." His words resonated with unsettling conviction.

        To be continued….

CHAPTER 16- SOIREE INCIDENT PT.7

The vehicle was a boxy, angular design, a stark, imposing shape. Atop its armored roof sat a rotary machine gun turret, its barrel menacingly prominent. The vehicle rode on large, aggressive off-road tires, promising superior traction and stability even on the roughest terrain.

Jermaine, surveying the devastation that had overtaken the city, let out a low whistle.

"Sheesh," he breathed.

The trunk door slid open, unveiling a hefty figure in a camouflage tactical jacket. His Afro, complete with a fro pick, and black leather gauntlet wristbands stood out against the chaotic parking lot.

"Come on in, boys," he said calmly, his sharp eyes scanning the scene.

"Where's the Inspector?" he inquired, his gaze sweeping for the familiar figures amid the disorder.

Noah stepped forward, his expression grim. "He stayed to fight Brooks."

The agent let out a short, humorless chuckle. "That dude's as good as dead."

Jermaine chuckled, a low rumble in his chest. "Brooks is kinda strong, though."

"Well," the agent replied, his tone laced with grudging respect, "the Inspector's stronger."

Malachi, gripping the car's reinforced bar, leaned in. "How's Deon doing?"

The agent's expression clouded with concern.

"I'm working on healing him," he said, voice tinged with uncertainty. "He's messed up pretty bad, but he's going to be alright."

Malachi turned from the jeep, gazing at the chaotic cityscape. "What the heck is going on?" he wondered aloud.

Suddenly, a sharp thwack echoed as Vance's combat machete struck the bulletproof window, sending cracks spidering through the glass.

Blood bloomed against the pane, a stark reminder of the unfolding chaos.

Malachi turned and saw Brooks standing at a broken window high in the hotel, the truth crashing down—Vance was dead. Noah's face filled with shock as he stared at Malachi, shouting, "Mal, wait!"

But Malachi had already yelled and taken off, leaving a rush of wind and chaos in his wake. His mind reeled, barely grasping the truth that Brooks had killed his godfather.

Noah narrowed his eyes, zeroing in on Brooks.

"Hold on... if he's here, does that mean you killed the inspector?"

Jermaine, standing nearby, shook his head in disbelief and said, "Did you see that? Malachi's on a whole other level right now."

At that moment, they watched Malachi drag Brooks down the hotel walls, the destruction marking their path like a scar in the air. The atmosphere grew dense and heavy, an unseen energy tingling across their skins.

Miguel appeared beside them, already engulfed in flames. The agent immediately said, "Miguel, your brother's losing it. Only you can calm him down before he causes more trouble."

Miguel sighed, a weary "No problem," escaping his lips before launching himself into the air, a fiery trailblazing in his wake, ascending towards the chaos above. Jermaine and Fabian exchanged surprised glances.

The agent explained, "Malachi's anger leaves a mark, a kind of spiritual scar. It's not just something he feels; it ripples outwards, affecting everyone around him."

Fabian questioned, "What kind of mark? Why does his anger affect us?"

The agent remarked, "You guys must've just awakened."

With a fiery streak blazing across the sky toward the hotel, the agent's voice was sharp with urgency.

He saw their lost expressions and continued, "Look, there's something called Spiritual Energy—it's like a life force, tied to everything we do and feel.

Some can control; we call them enlightened humans or the more fancy name Superhuman.

Malachi is one, and now so are you. His rage explodes this energy, leaving a spiritual scar."The group realized calming Malachi was crucial to stop his rage's physical toll on everyone.

Jermaine, curious, asked, "So, it's like using your soul?"

Before the agent could answer, a deafening *boom* from Malachi and Brooks' collision shattered glass and sent a shockwave through the parking lot, rattling nearby buildings. The chaos underscored their urgent mission to stabilize Malachi.

Dust and debris swirled around them as they landed in a chaotic heap of twisted metal and broken concrete.

Brooks, amidst the wreckage, let out a harsh laugh, the sound oddly defiant considering the circumstances.

Shadowy tendrils, thick as pythons, uncoiled from his body, rising like dark smoke from a smoldering pyre.

The valet placed his hands on the hood of a car, rolling his neck as the cuts on his skin slowly healed.

His voice was ragged with pain and exertion. "You need to slow down, damn it!"

Malachi, ignoring the throbbing in his own bruised knuckles, stood, his eyes narrowed. "After you're dead," he replied, his voice low and dangerous.

Shadow whips curled around the car as if alive, forming effortlessly from the valet's hands. With a wild laugh, the valet hurled the vehicle at Malachi.

As it flew towards him, Malachi met the car with a powerful punch, redirecting its trajectory back at the valet. The valet dove aside just in time, jabbing a finger at Malachi and shouting, "Boom!"

A dark streak of lightning crackled past Malachi, striking the hotel with a thunderous boom.

The glass shattered in an explosive symphony, and a burnt hole gaped ominously in the second-floor window, framed by licking flames. Glancing back at the destruction, Malachi quickly refocused his attention on the fight.

Brooks zipped towards him, but Malachi deftly weaved aside, maintaining a cold, intense glare.

As Brooks stumbled past, Malachi leaped, his foot crashing down mere moments after Brooks rolled out of the way. Brooks flipped up, his chuckle dying under Malachi's unwavering gaze. He tilted his head, a smirk twisting his lips. "Bro, you almost killed me."

"Don't call me 'bro'," Malachi snapped, irritation lacing his voice.
Malachi zipped to Brooks, delivering a rapid series of punches to his face. Black blood welled from Brooks' nose and mouth.

Brooks staggered, his chest bleeding, trickles of crimson beginning to stain his mouth. "God damn, boy," he wheezed, wincing from the impact. "The hell have they been feeding you?"

Without hesitation, Malachi seized Brooks by the face and slammed him into the ground with brutal force.

The earth cracked beneath the impact as Malachi relentlessly bashed his head into the ground, again and again, blood splattering with each vicious strike.
Flames erupted, engulfing nearby cars in a fiery blast before spreading rapidly.

Miguel emerged from the fire, his fiery hair now subdued, his expression grim.

"Hey, take it easy," Miguel urged.

"This bum killed Vance," Malachi shot back, rage simmering beneath his words. "The only other father figure we had left. And you expect to take it easy?"

Miguel held his gaze steady. "That's not how we do things. Besides, didn't God say vengeance is His? You don't want that blood on your hands."

Malachi paused, his gaze steady and cold. "God gave us these powers, didn't He? It's only right we use them to slay our demons."

Before the conversation could deepen, they both looked up, stunned by flashes and blasts echoing from the city.

Helicopters and gunfire filled the air. Miguel shook his head and asked, "Okay, what in God's name is going on now?"
A fierce wind erupted from Brooks, enveloping the brothers in its icy embrace and forcefully pushing the twins back.

Brooks lay on the ground, screaming in torment as his chest heaved, his body writhing with violent spasms of agony.

"Please, just end it!" he gasped, desperation dripping from every word. Clutching his chest, he struggled for each excruciating breath. "I'm begging you, Man, make it stop!"

Miguel turned to Malachi, urgency sharpening his voice. "Yo Mal, Stop the man is begging!"

Malachi looked at Miguel, his eyes filled with confusion and dread. "I'm not doing this," he whispered, a hint of fear in his voice.

Brooks held his face, yelling in agony as an unsettling transformation took hold. Malachi felt an evil presence ripple through the air, its dark energy pressing heavily on his senses.

The sound of bones cracking echoed ominously, causing Miguel to wince and make a face, his instinct to help clashing with caution.

Turning to Malachi, Miguel asked hesitantly, "Should we help him?" Malachi, shaken by the aura of malevolence emanating from Brooks, shook his head. "I don't know about that," he replied, uncertainty lacing his words.

As they watched, Brooks transformed, a guttural scream tearing from his throat as black blood erupted from his mouth.

A single, crimson horn curled from his forehead. His eyes became voids of black. His skin turned ashen grey, and his limbs hardened, ending in sharp, clawed hands. A long tail unfurled behind him, tipped with a deadly, red-tipped spike.

The transformation was accompanied by a violent convulsion, his body wracked with the effort of the change as he vomited more black blood.

He looked down at his clawed hands, flexing them with a chilling grace.

A chilling whisper, a breath on the nape of the neck, slithered directly into their mind: "Freedom."

The word hung in the air, heavy with promise, as the spiked tail unfurled behind the speaker, a menacing counterpoint to the seductive lure of power and control. A hiss followed, the word "At last" dripping with malicious intent, a promise of damnation.

The creature's gaze was sharp and analytical. He studied the brothers, weighing their strengths and weaknesses with cold precision.

"So, this is the pinnacle of human evolution?" he mused, his voice a low growl. "Mhmm. Intrigued," he said, the word betraying none of his true intentions.

His mind was already calculating strategies, plotting their demise or their potential use as tools.

To be continued...

CHAPTER 17- SOIREE INCIDENT PT.8

Miguel's eyes widened, his mouth agape as fear etched itself into his features. His breath came in quick, shallow gasps as he stammered, "What in the world is that ?"

The entity fixed its gaze skyward, a sinister smile playing on its lips as it spoke with chilling conviction. "This world festers in division. Its so-called protectors? Mere shadows. Soon, this realm will crumble, and all existence shall be ours," she declared, her voice dripping with malice. "Do you hear that, Father?"

Miguel stammered, "O-okay then. And who might—"

Before he could finish, the creature turned its hellish gaze upon him, its grotesque visage twisting into a sneer of disdain.

In a voice that rumbled like distant thunder, it proclaimed, "I am the embodiment of wrath. The harbinger of war. I am Azazel."

Miguel smirked, confidence radiating from his flaming fists. "Don't worry, bro, I got this," he declared, charging at Azazel with fiery determination. His punch landed, but the demon's retaliatory kick sent him crashing through a car with devastating force.

Malachi's eyes flared an intense blue, his shock quickly turning into resolve. He lunged at Azazel, but the demon effortlessly caught his leg. As Azazel slammed him into the ground, he sneered, "If this is the best mankind has to offer, you're in trouble." Pain coursed through Malachi's body, the demon's chilling words echoing in his mind.

Azazel then turned his unyielding gaze toward the hotel, his eyes dark and menacing, as if sensing the vibrations of fear and anticipation emanating from within its walls.

Noah charged in, resolve etched into his expression. With a sharp swipe of his hand, a massive hailstone descended, shattering with brutal precision against Azazel's temple.

Ice shards mixed with dark blood as Malachi sprang up with the agility of a ninja, unleashing a relentless series of punches into Azazel's stomach. Each hit drew forth more black blood as Malachi quipped with satisfaction, "Now, that's my best."

Jermaine appeared before them, his presence electric, braids gleaming white, arms marked with fierce tiger stripes. With a forceful double-palm thrust, he sent Azazel stumbling back.

Behind, Noah and Miguel restrained the demon, and Jermaine called to Malachi, "You and me," his gaze unwavering.

Malachi nodded in response, their combined assault fierce as Jermaine drove his claws into Azazel's chest, followed by Malachi's powerful uppercut that unleashed a geyser of dark blood.

Suddenly, Azazel's chest began to glow ominously. Malachi's eyes widened as he shouted, "Run!" They scattered just as Azazel erupted in an explosive burst, flinging Malachi into a hotel's column.

Groaning yet undeterred, he rose, ears ringing, to find Azazel advancing through the smoke.

A malevolent smirk twisted Azazel's lips as he spoke, his voice a chilling whisper, yet filled with dark amusement. "Do you know why my power eclipses yours?" he taunted, each word soaked in sinister intent.

"It's because humans today have grown soft, hiding behind their illusions of comfort. They've forgotten real strength."

His laughter echoed, cruel and resonant, as he moved with a predator's grace.

Malachi stood, frustration clear, a blue aura coating him as the ground cracked beneath his intensity

"I expected a goofy one-liner," he mocked Azazel. In an instant, Azazel lunged, but Malachi was ready, his fist driving into Azazel's chest. As Azazel reached for him, Malachi deftly backhanded the demon's hand and delivered a punishing blow to his side.

"Yo!" called a voice from the edge of the skirmish. Fabian appeared, arms glowing white.

He aimed his palm and unleashed a searing beam of light that crashed into Azazel, enveloping him in blinding radiance and staggering him backward.

Fabian erupted with excitement, "Let's go!" His joy was short-lived. In a flash, a fiery blur—Miguel—struck, knocking Fabian to the ground. Azazel swiftly seized Miguel, dragging him with terrifying force up the hotel's walls, leaving devastation in his path. Malachi stood, horror-stricken, as Fabian, on the ground, breathed a defeated "No."

In an instant, Azazel appeared beside Fabian, delivering a punishing blow that sprayed blood across the scene. Malachi turned just in time to see Azazel swallow a swirling ball of light, red lightning dancing across his skin. "Yeah, that's more like it," Azazel crowed with malevolent glee.

"You're a Shaka, aren't you? Why hold back those moon powers? I just devoured your friend's soul," he taunted, his laughter echoing ominously. "I'll feast on your friends' souls and save yours for last, to show you true power."

A noise interrupted them; Noah was rising, Azazel's attention shifting with a sneer. "You ready?" he mocked, the air thick with foreboding.

In a blur of motion, Azazel blitzed across the parking lot, slamming Noah against a wall, then a car, then finally, the unforgiving pavement.

Malachi watched in helpless horror as his friend was used as a human projectile.

Malachi clenched his fist, energy crackling around his knuckles. Azazel watched a flicker of genuine interest in his eyes.

He turned, adopting a fighting stance.

Azazel stood with arms spread wide, his voice dripping with malevolence as he taunted Malachi. "I hope you've had an eventful life, Malachi," he echoed mockingly.

"Because I'm going to tear your friends to shreds," he threatened, each word laced with wicked delight. "So, you better tap into that power of yours and kill me," he sneered, the glint of twisted amusement sparking in his eyes.

Malachi slapped his palm against his clenched fist, the sharp sound cutting through the tension. He offered a silent plea for God's strength, his anger simmering as Azazel's mocking presence taunted him, fueling his inner storm.

Azazel, a predatory grin on his face, aimed his palm at Malachi, preparing another attack. Malachi knew it was a fool's errand; Azazel was far faster, his reflexes lightning-quick.

But he had no choice. With a burst of adrenaline, Malachi zipped towards Azazel, moving with a speed that blurred his form—a supersonic dash, a desperate gamble.

As he moved, the same beam of reddish energy, erupted from Azazel's palm, aimed directly at Malachi's chest. The beam's passage scorched the ground, leaving a trail of molten earth and vaporized rock in its wake.

Malachi, caught in mid-movement, barely had time to react. He stopped abruptly, shielding his face with his arms as his body hummed with energy, a desperate attempt to enhance his defenses.

 He squeezed his eyes shut, bracing for the worst. A deafening clash of energy echoed around him.

When he opened his eyes shocked to see Jermaine stood with his back to the relentless force, his fangs bared in defiance, an agonized scream tearing through the chaotic air as the energy bore down upon him.

The force seized Jermaine, an electric jolt coursing through his body as his back miraculously healed, the wounds knitting together with a crackling surge of energy. Standing tall, a fierce light igniting in his eyes, Jermaine declared with unwavering determination, "We're going home tonight."

In a heartbeat, he vanished, a blur of motion streaking toward Azazel, his resolve as sharp and unyielding as a blade.

Simultaneously, Jermaine lunged, grabbing Azazel's arm with surprising strength. The fiery beam sputtered and died as Jermaine's grip tightened.

A transformation rippled across Jermaine's body; tiger stripes blazed across his skin, his eyes glowed with an eerie purple light, and fangs extended from his jaw. "Remember me?" he growled, his voice a low, guttural rumble.

Jermaine's claws barely pierced Azazel's chest. Azazel laughed, "Ha! I expected more from a beast like you," and drove his elbow down.

But Jermaine pivoted swiftly, delivering a sharp, upward strike to Azazel's jaw. Azazel's eyes widened in surprise, the impact reverberating through him as he staggered back.

Azazel casually brushed off his stomach, remarking with a smirk, "Humanity sure has developed some interesting abilities over sixteen hundred years."

Jermaine dropped into a beastly stance and yelled, "Come find out, then!" In an instant, Azazel flashed past Jermaine, grabbing his face and hurling him through the wall of the hotel with relentless force.

The impact shattered the wall, sending debris and dust exploding outward, leaving a gaping hole in the side of the building as Jermaine was flung into the chaos.

A sudden blur, followed by a metallic flash, interrupted Azazel's advance. His arm was slapped down with a forceful strike.

"What?" Azazel growled, eyeing Deon, who stood boldly with a menacing silver duel sickles in hand. "And who might this be?"

Nudging Malachi gently, Deon asked, "You good, bro?" Despite his mental turmoil, Malachi nodded, trying to project strength.

Before he could respond, a firm hand grasped his shoulder. Malachi turned to see the agent, his presence exuding calm authority. "I'm Agent Maxwell.

Mind if I form a bond with you? We need you at peak performance," he said, his voice soothing yet urgent.

Malachi, confused but hopeful, nodded as Maxwell focused intently. An indescribable sensation washed over him —like a gentle, refreshing breeze passing through his very soul.

As the bond formed, warmth spread through Malachi's body, his wounds mending, his spirit-lifting.

Calm serenity filled him, dispelling the chaos inside his mind, and for the first time, he felt ready to face the monstrous force that threatened them all.

Deon stepped forward with confidence, twirling his dual sickles with ease. "What do you say, cuz?" he called out, his grin sharp and daring.

How about we put our differences aside and kill this... thing?"

Malachi's gaze remained locked on Azazel, his fists clenched tightly. "Alright," he declared, his voice a steady resolve.

Azazel's roar filled the air, incredulity lacing his words. "A thing? Do you dare call me a thing? I am a god!"

Without missing a beat, Deon arched an eyebrow, smirking. "What did you just say?"

Before Azazel could respond, Maxwell stepped forward, placing a hand on Malachi and Deon's backs.

Maxwell was an imposing figure, his robust form hinting at unexpected agility. Orbs with lines formed around his mesmerizing eyes.

A vibrant purple field enveloped the three, its edges crackling with energy. Within this field, Malachi and Deon felt a surge of power, their muscles tensing with newfound strength, their senses sharpening, and their resolve hardening.

The intensity of their emotions amplified, a focused calm replacing any previous uncertainty.

The field itself pulsed with the energy, a tangible manifestation of Maxwell's power, before slowly fading as the amplified abilities settled within them.

In a blur, Azazel zipped toward them, a dark force of nature. Malachi caught sight of the oncoming threat, adrenaline sharpening his senses.

Just as Azazel closed in, Deon moved with blinding speed and precision. His sickle slashed upward, cleaving through Azazel's chest.

Black blood sprayed into the air, viscous and dark as night, painting the ground with unholy ichor.

Azazel staggered back, astonishment etched across his features. He clutched his chest, black blood seeping through his fingers.

Deon, smirking, taunted him, "What do you think you're doing?"

                                    To be continued.

CHAPTER 18- SOIRÉE INCIDENT PT.9

Azazel stood, momentarily lost in thought, as Malachi and Deon exchanged tense glances. Then, a wicked grin spread across his face.

"So, mankind hasn't grown weaker over the years," he mused with a dark thrill. "Good. At least I'll have a bit of sport before I devour your souls and achieve omniscience."

Deon thrust his sickle at Azazel, but the demon caught it effortlessly.

As Deon staggered from Azazel's punch to his gut, Malachi grabbed the sickle, slicing through Azazel's palm and spilling black blood that hissed upon touching the ground.

Malachi swung again, but Azazel ducked beneath, his tail carving a deep gouge in the earth as it missed Malachi by inches.

Deon intercepted the tail just in time, a silvery light flaring in his other hand as he formed a luminous lunar javelin.

He hurled it at Azazel, and the ensuing explosion tore through the battlefield, shattering stones and raining debris.

Black blood spattered from the blast, leaving a smoldering crater in Azazel's wake. The force of the extraction was so great it cleanly severed Azazel's hand at the wrist.

As the smoke from the blast cleared, Deon waved it away. The sickle in Malachi's hand crackled, sending silver streams toward Deon.

"Is he dead?" Malachi asked, tense with anticipation. Deon sucked his teeth. "It's gonna take us and Christ himself to win this," he replied grimly.

Feeling a rush of spiritual energy, Malachi said, "Even when I'm deep in the trenches, I won't fear a thing," as an electric buzz steadied his resolve.

Just then, a shadow leaped from the crater—Azazel landed before them with a fearsome snarl.

Deon held his gun finger aimed at Azazel, a fierce determination in his eyes. Suddenly, a mini comet flared to life, its tail shimmering brightly as it shot toward the demon. Azazel, unfazed, held his arms out wide, a dark aura swirling around him.

With a swift motion, he swiped his arm, and a massive dark orb closed around the incoming projectile, swallowing it whole. The orb pulsed with energy, its surface rippling as it absorbed the comet's brilliance. Then, with a powerful thrust, Azazel sent the orb soaring into the air.

As it reached its peak, the orb exploded in a cataclysmic burst, sending tendrils of darkness spiraling outwards, contrasting sharply with the remnants of light. The shockwave rippled through the air, leaving behind a haunting silence in the wake of the explosive display.

Malachi charged through the whirling dust, landing powerful blows on the demon.

Each strike sent shockwaves of pain through Azazel, who struggled to catch Malachi.

Roaring, Azazel stomped the ground, sending a shockwave that blasted both the dust and Malachi away.

The earth cracked under the impact as Malachi was flung backward, crashing into the rear windshield of a car.

"Mal, you good?" Deon yelled. Malachi rolled off the car, looking dazed but determined. "What is he doing?" he asked, eyes fixed on Azazel's next move.

Azazel knelt, a soft chuckle escaping his lips. Malachi and Deon exchanged anxious glances. "I owe you an apology," Azazel said, his tone unexpectedly soft. "I took you too lightly. I should've known better—you're Shaka's, after all." His words carried a weight that lingered in the air.

He raised his hand, pointing towards the night sky. The ground cracked loudly beneath them; fissures branched across the asphalt.

Malachi and Deon wavered, struggling to regain their balance. In an instant, Deon shimmered into view beside Malachi, a sudden burst of moonlit brilliance enveloping them both.

Gripping Malachi's arm, Deon whisked them across the battlefield in the blink of an eye, materializing at Maxwell's side. Maxwell's voice cut through the air, sharp and commanding, "Brace yourselves."

From the earth's wounds, thermal energy surged upwards like a fiery river, coalescing into a blazing supernova—a furious orb of blue-white fire against the night. It pulsed with terrifying power, cars melting like wax and buildings aflame, heat unbearable and all-consuming.

Despite the inferno, Maxwell's healing held, though strained. Clothes ignited but burns healed instantly.

Malachi shielded his face, clothing reduced to ash. Deon's steady grip reassured them. "Ready for a dip?" he whispered above the chaos.

Maxwell, disoriented, blinked. "Huh?"

"We're teleporting to the ocean," Deon murmured urgently. "This thing's strong enough to wipe Jamaica off the map."

Flames burst atop the hotel, casting an intense glow. Malachi and the others looked up, spotting Miguel against the fiery backdrop—a beacon of hope that filled Malachi with relief.

Maxwell exhaled softly, a smile spreading across his face. "God is really on your side. Welcome back, man," he said warmly.

Azazel traced the sky with a grim smile. "You're alive... what a complication."

Miguel soared through the night sky, a captivating figure silhouetted against the darkness, as blue flames erupted from his palms, propelling him upward.
A brilliant azure light trailed him like a celestial flare, casting a shimmering aura before he met the earth with a resounding embrace.

Maxwell stood among them, an aura of quiet confidence illuminating his presence. Turning to Deon, he spoke with a gentle certainty.

"I'm about to attempt the greatest amplification and healing I've ever done."

Deon, apprehension shadowing his voice, asked, "Is it ...safe?"

Maxwell's calm smile lingered. "No, it might fry my mind. But it's worth it."

As his eyes fluttered closed, Maxwell focused, the delicate lines around them multiplying into radiant purple patterns that glowed softly across the parking lot.

He interlocked his hands upside down, his focus unyielding. "Quantum entanglement," he announced firmly. He made a decisive adjustment, continuing, "Let's extend the reach—700 feet in front of me."

Upon his utterance, violet lines emerged, flowing seamlessly over his body and cascading to the ground below.

These lines unfurled across the parking lot, creating an elaborate lattice of interconnected dots and strands.

As they stretched outward, they formed a complex network, all connected except for a clear boundary that parted around Azazel, avoiding him entirely.

 In this moment of enchanted warmth, Malachi felt a profound surge within him.

Yet, mingling with the newfound strength, a realization blossomed—a quiet acknowledgment of his frailty compared to their power.

Even as the warmth infused him, Malachi's thoughts danced between admiration and a yearning to grasp the strength they wielded so effortlessly.

Nevertheless, nestled within the radiant glow of Maxwell's selfless act was the promise of growth—a hope that he too could one day harness such enchanting power.

To be continued...

CHAPTER 19- SOIRÉE INCIDENT PT.10

Miguel's rock-hewn arm firmly gripped the crater's edge, the ethereal blue flames weaving around him like a protective veil.

Azazel watched, his gaze a captivating mix of disbelief and curious intrigue. With a steady determination, Miguel crawled out of the smoking crater, the mesmerizing flames casting a softly glowing aura around him, illuminating his every movement.

Azazel turned to Miguel, a curious glint in his eye. "Did you absorb all of that?" he asked, his voice low and gravelly.

Miguel shook his head, coughing blood. Before he could answer, silver light flashed, and Malachi and Deon materialized beside him, flanking Miguel protectively.

Deon's silver scythe rested casually on his shoulder. Facing Azazel, they stood poised and ready. Azazel casually glanced back over his shoulder, a slight smirk playing on his lips as his eyes fell upon Maxwell, a few feet away, his hands locked together in a familiar stance.

"Welcome back, young man," Deon said with a nod to Miguel, eyeing his arm curiously. "What's up with that?"

Miguel glanced at his rocky arm with a chuckle. "I honestly thought I was done for. Looks like it healed this way," he said, flexing the stone-like appendage.

The trio assumed fighting stances—Deon with his weapon, Malachi and Miguel's fists raised. "Alright, let's do this," Miguel declared.

Azazel sneered, "Kill me? We'll see."

Miguel zipped toward him, unleashing a devastating combo culminating in a fiery fist. The blast pushed Azazel back, but he stood defiant.

"My father should never have created humanity," he roared, "I will purge them from this realm! They're like insects trying to stop a global catastrophe!"

Azazel moved like a phantom, a blur of motion aimed at Miguel. Deon reacted instantly, the scythe's blade meeting Azazel's fist with a shower of sparks.

Before the dust settled, Malachi unleashed a devastating axe kick, pulverizing the earth. Yet, Azazel's fist punched through the debris, connecting with Deon's jaw. Deon reeled back, Miguel's warning barely audible over the roar of the impact.

Miguel pulled Malachi clear as Azazel's roundhouse kick, a whirlwind of claws and fury, whistled past.

"Your feeble attempts amuse me," Azazel taunted. "Your powers are meaningless."

Miguel responded swiftly, his punch sending blue flames streaking toward Azazel. Upon impact, the flames erupted with devastating force, causing shockwaves that shattered windows and splintered nearby structures. Debris was cast into the air as the ground trembled under the unleashed energy's power.

The blast hurled Malachi into a wrecked car. He staggered out, blood streaming from his face, his eyes blazing with fury.

Malachi saw Azazel blitzing toward Maxwell, the chilling words "Goodbye, you're becoming bothersome" slicing through the air. "No!" Malachi screamed.

Miguel came running, his voice a shout urging Malachi to escape, before unleashing a fiery projectile from his mouth.

The fire projectile seared a deep gash into Azazel's side, eliciting a roar of pain. But before the onlookers could react, the wound vanished, the flesh knitting itself back together.

"Insolent whelp!" Azazel thundered, his gaze fixed on Miguel. The eerie purple cracks in the ground slowly faded, leaving behind only dust and debris. Maxwell crumpled to the ground, his face striking the earth.

Malachi's voice was a groan of disbelief, "You've got to be kidding me." But before Malachi could respond, Miguel shot forward, air shimmering from the intense heat he emitted.

The scorching temperature forced Malachi to shield his eyes. Miguel zipped past Azazel, his fiery presence a searing torrent, and unleashed a crackling, roaring blast.

Hovering in the air, Miguel narrowly dodged Azazel's spiked tail. He held both hands toward Azazel, energy building between them, but Azazel vanished.

Suddenly, Azazel appeared behind Miguel, kicking him into a cluster of cars that exploded upon impact.

The nightmare replayed: Miguel's frantic assault, Azazel's impossible speed, the cataclysmic clash.

The impossible spectacle shattered Malachi's world, not from violence alone, but through its sheer defiance of logic. The unbridled power and speed tore apart reality as he knew it, breaking the chains of his limitations and unleashing something primal.

In an instant, a flood of untamed energy coursed through him. The crushing weight of his father's death and relentless training transformed into strengths, forging an unbreakable core.

Weakness and doubt vanished, replaced by vibrant awareness. The world sharpened into clarity; colors intensified, unveiling hidden details. His amber eyes flared to electric blue, radiating an intense, inner light.

Feeling the world, not just seeing it, he sensed air shifts, temperature changes, and energy currents—a symphony he began to understand. The world became a canvas awaiting his mark; this awakening was a revelation. He was no longer just Malachi; he was becoming more.

Gusts swirled around Azazel, an eerie smile playing on his lips. "So, this is the spiritual awakening I've heard about," he mused.

Blue lightning erupted from the air around Malachi, the earth exploding under the impact of the devastating bolts. Debris rained down as energy crackled and surged.

At that moment, the whites of Malachi's eyes turned silvery, his irises glowing with an intense blue.

The darkness peeled away, revealing the world around him in sharp, vivid detail, every shadow and crevice laid bare. Azazel watched with a thrill of anticipation at the raw power unleashed before him.

Breathless, Malachi clutched his chest, struggling to find air as the energy storm began to subside. As calm settled in, he slowly regained his composure. He lifted his gaze to Azazel, eyes blazing with fierce determination.

"One of us will die," Malachi declared with unwavering resolve, "and it won't be me."

Azazel chuckled, anticipation gleaming in his eyes. "Finally, it's me who faces the world of men. This is the battle I've awaited. I knew saving you for last would be worthwhile..." His voice carried a hint of disappointment.

"A shame I won't witness more of the Shaka's lunar powers." With fluid grace, he slipped into a stance, eager for the thrill ahead.

Azazel charged toward Malachi with fierce intent. In a silver blur, Deon appeared from the side and deftly shoved Azazel aside, redirecting the demon's path with swift precision.

"How's my timing?" Deon asked.

Malachi grunted, "Mh."

Deon jerked his head back, eyes widening. "Whoa! I dig the eyes," he said, taking in the unexpected glow.

Before he could react, Azazel's spiked tail slammed into Deon's leg, a spray of gore marking the brutal impact.

Deon groaned, but even as he swiped upward, a silver light enveloped him; his shield shifting, reforming into an ikakalaka sword.

With a swift, upward slash, he cleaved Azazel's chin, the demon roaring in pain and surprise.

Seizing the opportunity, Azazel ripped his tail free from Deon's leg and plunged it deep into Deon's shoulder.

Malachi seized the sword and, with a swift slice, severed Azazel's thrashing tail. Black blood gushed out, pooling on the ground and permeating the air with a funeral-like scent.

Azazel roared, "You dare?!" black blood spurted as he spun. Then, everything went black for Malachi.

Malachi opened his eyes to a searing pain in his chest. Azazel stood over him, Deon slumped in his grasp.

Azazel took a long, slow sniff of Deon, his nostrils flaring as silvery energy flowed visibly from Deon into him.

Malachi surged to his feet, a fist crashing into Azazel's jaw. The demon slid a few feet back.

Malachi caught Deon as he collapsed, cradling him gently. Deon's skin was pale, his eyes closed, and his lips cracked and dry. Malachi laid him down carefully.

"Well, look who's still standing," Azazel rasped, wiping the blood from his mouth with a dark grin. "Did some divine fool decide to protect you? Not that it'll matter in the end."

Malachi stood firm, meeting Azazel's gaze. "Is Brooks still in there?" he asked, his voice carrying an edge.

Azazel's expression darkened with anger. "It's my body now!" he retorted sharply, his voice rising with frustration. "Brooks is dead!" he shouted, making his point with a final, emphatic yell.

Azazel erupted in a furious tirade. "It's my body now! Brooks is dead! Gone! Understand?!" His voice cracked with a mixture of rage and something akin to grief. It was then Malachi glanced down, feeling a sharp tug of pain.

Malachi's skepticism only deepened. If Brooks was truly gone, then what were these radiant souls he perceived? Azazel's words rang hollow, cloaking an uncomfortable truth.

Azazel sneered, "Why don't you just shut your trap, kid? I'm going to rip out your soul, savor it like a fine feast, and then dismantle your friends in ways that will redefine gruesomely."

The demon surged forward, a blur of motion cracking the earth beneath him.

Malachi felt his fists ignite with power, the Spiritual Energy surging through him effortlessly.

He reared back and struck, his punch slamming into Azazel's chin with a resounding crack.

Azazel's head jerked upward from a powerful uppercut, spraying an arc of black blood into the air. "You think this will stop me?"

The next strike hit him in the stomach with relentless precision, sending a spray of dark ichor up from his back. "Is that all you've got?" He taunted.

As Malachi's blows landed, cracks began forming on Azazel's form, each strike threatening to break him apart. "You're barely making a dent," he jeered, trying to mask his concern with bravado.

His strikes were causing more than physical damage, and the realization intrigued him.

The energy from the strike overturned nearby cars and scattered debris. Azazel, off-balance and infuriated, felt a rising apprehension as he faced the formidable power Malachi wielded.

Azazel smirked, his eyes glinting with a dark amusement.

"Surely, this can't still be the feeble mortal they call Malachi," he taunted, his voice dripping with disdain. "Show me, then, what you're truly made of."

His smile widened, a challenge etched into every feature, as Malachi stood up, his form flickering like a mirage in the desert sun.

Instinctively, Azazel stepped back, bracing himself as Malachi reappeared, jabbing with calculated precision.

Azazel caught the strike with both palms, the force rippling through his body like a shockwave, muscles tensing, veins bulging, eyes narrowing as if warding off multiple unseen blows.

Azazel staggered, a cruel smile twisting his lips.

"Foolish mortal," he hissed, "You have no idea what you've done."

He brought his hands together in a complex gesture, the fingers of his right hand overlapping those of his left in a precise pattern.

Shadows erupted from him, swirling and coiling around his feet, snaking across the ground like living things.

Then, with a deafening roar, the ground exploded outwards in a violent eruption of earth and rock.

Malachi shielded his face, the force of the blast throwing him backward.

He reacted instantly, a shimmering, translucent barrier rippling into existence around him – an air wall, a dome of protective energy that enveloped him completely.

Malachi's eyes widened. He was no longer in the same place. The familiar landscape was gone, replaced by a scene of stark, alien beauty.

A red sun hung low in the sky, casting long, eerie shadows across a shallow black lake. Towering mountains, their peaks shrouded in mist, encircled the still, dark water.

It had to be some kind of illusion, a mind trick... but the smell of damp earth and the icy touch of the black water were undeniably real.

The red sun beat down on him, a tangible heat on his skin. This felt too real to be a mere illusion.

Yet, a resolve flickered within him. Running a hand over his mouth, he braced himself for whatever challenges lurked in the eerie world ahead.

The water rippled ominously as Malachi turned to see Azazel emerge, his expression a mixture of disdain and inevitability.

"I know you're wondering why a god would target your kind," Azazel began, his voice resonant and edged with urgency, echoing like thunder across the heavens.

He knelt by the river of shadow, its waters dark as the void, and with a solemn grace, he scooped up a handful. The liquid shimmered in the crimson glow, akin to the blood of the covenant, as he drank it down in a single, swift gulp.

"But understand," he continued, his eyes aflame with a divine fervor, "we do this to save ourselves, as Noah built the ark to weather the flood, as Moses parted the sea to lead his people to salvation.

It is written in the scrolls of destiny, a trial by fire to purify and renew. For in the end, it is not wrath but redemption that guides our hand."

The power hidden within your soul is the key. With it, we will ignite a second war in heaven."

Azazel's form contorted into a nightmarish visage. His demonic goat's head, crowned with arm-length, twisted horns, sat above a body of coarse black fur and rock-like skin, glowing with inner flames.

Hooves struck with ominous finality, and his serpentine tail trailed behind. His eyes, black voids of burning intensity, cast a malevolent glow. "I shall rectify this divine misstep, erasing your kind," he declared, voice filled with chilling certainty.

Malachi held his gaze, thoughts drifting to the good book and its tales of demonic envy.

Now, the reality stood before him, more terrifying than any scripture could convey.

Azazel slammed his hand into the water, sending a spray of droplets cascading around him.

"Eminent One," Azazel praised, his voice low and intense, filled with pride. "It is with great respect that I bestow this title upon you."

"You and your bloodline... you've done what no other mortal has ever accomplished.

You've forced me to reveal the full extent of my power." He paused, a shadow crossing his face.

"Samyaza... he'd laugh, I'm sure. But he wouldn't understand the depth of your ancestor's legacy, the weight of the name I've given you."

To be continued...

CHAPTER 20- SOIREE INCIDENT FINAL. PT

Malachi stared at Azazel, doubts, and questions gathering like storm clouds. Was this monstrous form Azazel's true self, or a desperate transformation to survive their battle? Azazel caught Malachi's contemplative gaze, a mocking grin twisting his face into something terrifying. "What's wrong, Shaka? Got something to say?"

With a casual shrug, Malachi let a smirk dance on his lips. "Nah, just thinking of ways to kill you."

Azazel's laughter rang out, sharp and dripping with arrogance. "Kill me? I'm a celestial, incapable of being killed. But you, you're just dirt."

Without a moment's hesitation, Malachi retorted, "Yeah, but I was made from dirt in the image and likeness of God."

Azazel, his face a mask of furious rage, roared, "Silence!" he aimed his palm directly at Malachi, and tendrils of inky black water shot forth, impossibly fast.

They lashed out, wrapping around Malachi's arm and clamping over his mouth, while others snaked around his head, constricting him. Malachi struggled, pulling against the suffocating tendrils, but they held firm.

Azazel laughed, a sound like stones grinding together. "This is my world, mortal," he sneered, his voice echoing across the desolate landscape. "Here, I am god, and I can kill you with a thought."

But Malachi's eyes burned with defiance. His sword flared into existence, a blade of pure, solidified spiritual energy – a testament to the years he'd spent honing his abilities after abolishing his family's inherited powers. With a powerful backhand swing, he slashed through the tendrils of black water, severing them with surprising ease.

Azazel's laughter ceased abruptly. His eyes narrowed, a flicker of genuine surprise crossing his features. "I... I am surprised," he admitted, his voice laced with grudging respect. "You may be the first human I've encountered that I might... tolerate."

Malachi zipped toward Azazel with blinding speed, his sword a mere blur. Azazel reacted instantly, blocking the fierce chop with his forearm. Sparks erupted as the power-charged blade lodged into Azazel's fiery goat skin. His blazing eyes widened in surprise, and thick, black blood oozed from the cut, a testament to the sword's deadly edge.

Before Malachi could follow up, Azazel lashed out with his other hand. A second sword, this one formed from swirling black water, shot upward with terrifying speed. It spun a deadly vortex of darkness and slashed across Malachi's left eye.

Malachi stumbled back, clutching at his bleeding eye, a cry of pain and fury tearing from his throat. His sword, momentarily forgotten in the chaos, vanished in a flash of blue lightning, leaving him vulnerable and enraged.

In a blink, Azazel appeared, a swirling black-water sword, crimson-flashed and writhing like a living thing, hovering over his shoulder. Its edges were ragged and unpredictable, a terrifyingly fluid and powerful weapon.

His hand closed around Malachi's throat with an unrelenting grip.

Malachi's vision blurred with crimson and darkness, as Azazel leaned in, the chilling finality in his voice echoing, "This is the end of your life."

Suddenly the air around them wavered as the world was slit between them from the sky to the ground between them, then crumpled away.

In an instant, they were back in the ruined parking lot, reality reasserting itself.

As Azazel processed what had happened, a shimmering white blade pierced his chest from behind, its force driving the metal clean through him.

Black blood spilled from Azazel's mouth as he staggered, eyes wide in disbelief at the blade impaling him. His grip faltered, and he dropped Malachi, who clutched his bleeding eye, a long vertical scar slashing across it.

She was a girl with braids, her long-sleeved black dress swaying as she moved, face streaked with blood. With calm resolve, she swiped her white marine combat sword upward, cleaving through a shoulder. Blood spattered as she wiped the blade clean against her forearm.

Beside her stood a muscular man with wavy hair, his suit bloodied and marked with slashes.

His eyes, orange, bore into Azazel with fierce intensity, a fresh slash crisscrossing his nose bridge. "Maria, seal this vagabond!" he commanded, his voice booming with authority.

Malachi recognized the braided hair girl, Catherine, as she twirled her sword effortlessly.

Lastly, a brown-skinned woman stood before them, her blonde afro contrasting strikingly against her glowing white eyes.

Clad in a sparkling black dress, she seemed to be around Malachi's age.

Behind her, a purple portal hovered with an ethereal shimmer. In a blur of motion, Catherine darted at Azazel, a flash of white slicing through the chaos as she cleaved his jaw open.

Azazel pulled back, laughter spilling from him as his wound healed swiftly.

Yet Malachi noticed something vital—even as he clutched his bleeding stomach, he saw that while Azazel's jaw had mended, the wound on his stomach remained grievously open.

Azazel sneered, attempting to weaken their spirits with condescending taunts. "Women should be at home, not on the battlefield," he mocked. The women remained unfazed, exchanging knowing glances. One smirked and shot back, "Interesting, considering you can't handle us excelling at both."

The other man, Jordan, nodded to the white-eyed girl. "Maria, do you mind?" he asked.

"Gladly," Maria replied, a sly smile touching her lips as she clapped her hands together. In an instant, giant purple hands materialized in the air, mirroring her action.

They slammed together with force, enveloping Azazel in a shimmering purple orb, trapping him within its mystical confines.

Azazel continued his relentless assault against the walls of his prison. "Let me out!" he roared, his voice a crescendo of futile anger.

"Jordan," Azazel called enticingly, "I know about your son. Secrets await if you free me."

Catherine advanced, weapon poised for a decisive strike. "Don't trust a word he says!" Her voice was as sharp as her blade. "A demon twists truth into chains that bind us."

Maria's voice cut through the chaos, urgent and strained. "I can't hold him any longer! You need to call it in now!" As she spoke, blood began to trickle from her nose and mouth, underscoring the desperation of her plea.

As Azazel unleashed a furious scream, Malachi caught Catherine's eye. He recognized her stance instantly—a lethal readiness he had come to know all too well.

He gripped her hand in quiet support, a shared moment of resolve. Catherine nodded, her gaze a steadying beacon as she turned to Jordan. Her look spoke volumes, a silent bulwark against the chaos.

Jordan, bolstered by their unspoken pact, lifted his wrist device. "We've got him. Do it, do it now!" he declared, his voice firm.

"Copy," came the quick response, as Azazel's fate was sealed, their unity and strength woven into every action and word.

Suddenly, multiple beams of light descended from the sky. One struck Azazel directly, engulfing him in a brilliant flash, while others streaked across the city, lighting up the horizon with their distant impacts.

As Azazel was consumed by the radiant force, two piercing screams echoed through the air—one unmistakably Azazel's, filled with fury and agony, and the other a human cry, raw and terrified. With a final, resounding crack, Azazel shattered and vanished, leaving only a faint afterglow behind.

Malachi shielded his face from the blinding light, peering through his fingers as he wondered if it finally killed Azazel.

After the dust settled and the chaos subsided, the city lay still, its skyline dotted with fading lights from the strike.

In the aftermath, Catherine embraced Jordan, offering solace amidst the ruins of battle. As she hugged him, her eyes met Malachi's, whose crescent eye shifted to a warm amber brown. Malachi touched his scarred face and winced, staring at the blood on his fingers. "Is that all it took to kill him?" he asked, his voice a mix of hope and skepticism.

Maria shook her head with a weary sigh. "I wish," she replied. "No, we just sent him back to hell.".

She stepped back, sorrow in her eyes as she saw his damaged eye. "I'm sorry I didn't arrive sooner," she whispered, pulling him back into a comforting embrace.

Malachi reassured her, "It's alright. We survived. And from the looks of things, we weren't alone in facing a demon."

Concern flickered on her face. "What about Miguel?"

He looked around the chaos. "I think he's alive, at least I hope," he confessed, a trace of guilt in his voice. "I feel like it's my fault."

She met his gaze, gentle and understanding. "Why do you think that?" she asked, ready to share the weight of his guilt as always.
Malachi shrugged, playing it cool. Jordan approached, sincerity etched on his face. "I'm serious, Malachi. You holding your ground made all the difference for us. We owe you." His words carried the weight of genuine gratitude.

"By God's grace, I'm still standing," Malachi said, nodding gratefully to his comrades.

Maria nodded. "Amen to that."

Jordan asked about the agents, and Malachi's response was grim. "They did, but they're all dead."

Jordan sighed. "What about Inspector Vance?"

A shadow flickered across Malachi's face as he shook his head. Catherine's expression crumpled, tears welling as she covered her mouth.

"I'm so sorry," Maria whispered to Malachi and Catherine.

Maria approached Malachi, asking softly, "Mind if I?" He nodded. As her hand touched his bleeding stomach, the wound healed, and Malachi realized he'd never noticed the cut.

As Maria held her hand there, warmth spread, and the wounds healed, leaving faint scars. "Sorry," she said tiredly. "If I wasn't so drained, I could've healed them completely."

The pain, the searing agony behind his left eye, receded like a tide going out. He marveled at her touch, a feeling of profound relief washing over him. "Whoa," he breathed, but then he noticed something.

The deep claw marks that had gouged his flesh and taken his sight weren't healing. They remained as stark reminders of the fight and Azazel's power. The pain had faded, but the scars lingered.

A purple light flickered briefly before sputtering out. Startled by this unexpected failure, Malachi pulled away, still grateful for the healing she had achieved.
Maria stared at her palm, puzzled. "I can't heal it," she said, disbelief in her voice.

Jordan frowned, confused. "What do you mean you can't heal it?"

The bruised sun rose over the highway carnage. Malachi leaned against a battered ambulance, his left eye a swollen mess beneath hastily applied bandages. Each touch from the paramedic sent jolts of pain.

He accepted fresh bandages, mumbled a thank you, and watched her move on to tend to others, the rising sun offering little solace.

Climbing into the back of the ambulance, Malachi sat next to Miguel, who lay on a stretcher, his arms folded across his chest as he stared at the roof of the vehicle.

Miguel glanced at Malachi's bandaged eye and smirked, "You look a mess."

Malachi chuckled, "You don't look so bad yourself."

Miguel raised his bandaged hand, grimacing. "Yeah, my arm's turned to rock, and I have no idea why—I'm all love."

His statement drew laughter from Malachi, and they shared a moment of camaraderie before Miguel folded his arms, both of them reflecting on the night's events.

Malachi surveyed the destroyed parking lot and the half-standing hotel. Amidst the chaos, he found a glimmer of hope. "Well, at least we made it through," he remarked.

Their conversation took a serious turn as Miguel sighed and apologized. "I'm sorry I wasn't much help tonight."

"What are you talking about?" Malachi said. "You absorbed that... fire ring thing... and saved us all. I might not fully get where you're coming from, but I'm with you. Next time, it's you and me handling it."

Grasping Miguel's hand, Malachi made his vow. Miguel met his gaze and said, "No matter what happens, you're my brother for life."

To be continued...

CHAPTER 21- TRANQUIL

An hour later, the twins found themselves seated in a state-of-the-art conference room at the JDF headquarters.

The space was sleek and futuristic, with walls that doubled as digital displays, currently set to a soothing azure.

The room exuded an air of high-tech sophistication, perfectly calibrated to stimulate focus and intrigue.

Across from them sat Captain Mark, his demeanor as solid as the steel accents of the room, and Captain Renee, whose striking white pixie-cut hair was a bright contrast to her elegant blue dress—a modern splash of color against the technical backdrop.

Mark slapped a thick file onto the table with a grin. "Alright, so here's the deal. These are records of some seriously weird stuff happening all over the world. We've been keeping tabs for about six months now."

Renee leaned in, her voice calm but firm. "What happened tonight? It's no coincidence."

Miguel sighed deeply, running a hand through his hair. "Yeah, Brooks told me that hell's gates are wide open."

Mark shook his head, looking thoughtful. "Not quite. The gates are sealed, but there's a small breach," he said, adding confidently, "I know that for sure."

Just enough for Azazel and his crew to slip through. How they pulled it off is a mystery.

But I've got a gut feeling that something huge is brewing. If we don't get to the bottom of this before they strike again, we're in big trouble. And we've already lost some good people."

Malachi winced, rubbing his throbbing temple. "Azazel... he said they've been planning this for sixteen hundred years. Said it was to save themselves. Something about... a second war in Heaven." He shrugged, the gesture weak and unconvincing.

Miguel whistled low, shaking his head. "You're kidding. The Prince of Darkness is our ops? I can't believe it.

Don't get me wrong, the battle's always been against principalities and powers, but we're literally *boxing* with these guys."

Mark's eyes met the brothers', his usually cheerful demeanor now touched with a rare seriousness. "So, what do you say? Are you ready to save humanity?"

Miguel paused, concern clouding his features. "What about the others who fought alongside us?"

Mark leaned back, his whole demeanor shifting as he exhaled heavily, the weight of the situation more palpable than the unlit cigarette he removed from his lips.

"Deon's in recovery at the mansion, Jermaine's up and moving, and Noah's at your family's place, slowly healing.

Agent Maxwell is alive but trapped in a coma." His voice cracked, eyes shadowed with grief. "And... we lost Fabian."

Miguel's voice was a whisper as he looked up, saying, "What?"

Malachi felt the news like a punch. He had saved Fabian, and Fabian had saved him, but when Azazel came, he couldn't help him. Guilt gnawed at him; he had liked and respected Fabian deeply. The sense of failure was suffocating, overshadowing his grief.

Mark leaned back in the sleek, high-tech chair, the cool leather a contrast to the sweat still clinging to his skin.

Malachi's gaze dropped to his hands, thumbs twisting anxiously around each other. "I made a promise to save them," he murmured, a tremor in his voice. "But I failed."

He looked up at Mark, determination hardening his features. "With demons threatening our world, my family, and my friends, you bet I'm in."

Miguel nodded in Malachi's direction and said, "What he said."
Mark clapped his hands together, letting out a triumphant laugh. "Great! Welcome aboard!"

Renee stilled the room with a steady voice, cutting through the buzz. "Before we go any further, Malachi, what was Azazel truly after? Aside from the obvious threats."

Malachi ran a hand through his hair, weariness in his eye. "He kept going on about proving to God that creating us was a mistake. It's like he's obsessed with showing we're not worth the effort."

Malachi hesitated, then added, "He also mentioned that I remind him of one of my ancestors of mine ."

Renee leaned in, curiosity piqued. "Did he say a name?"

Malachi thought for a moment, then shook his head, deciding against revealing too much. "Nah, he didn't," he replied, keeping the name of his ancestor—someone he'd recently learned about—close to his chest.

When they finally got home, Malachi reached the stone steps and paused to enter the key code.

He felt his hand tremble slightly as Miguel, walking behind him with a crutch, teased, "You forgot it, didn't you?" Malachi chuckled, "Nah, nah," and keyed it in. They stepped inside.

The living room was familiar, with its black sofas circling warmly around the space.

A staircase wound its way up behind the rightmost sofa, where Bianca, their mom, sat.

Across from her, Dre, their best friend, sat with his head down, his hair in a fade peeking from beneath a cream hoodie.

When he looked up, his face was marked by bandages: one over his right eye, others on his nose and right cheek. Beside him, their sister slept in a playpen.

Mrs. Shaka stood up quickly, rushing over to them with tears in her eyes. "I was so worried," she cried as she embraced them tightly.

Malachi looked over at Bianca, seeing her press her lips together as their mom slowly released them.

Then Bianca hugged them too, tears streaming down once more. Dre approached, and they all joined in another group hug, momentarily soaking in the relief of being together again.

Once they were settled, Malachi gently brushed his baby sister's locs from her face, her light skin glowing softly in the dim light as she slept.

Meanwhile, Miguel sat with Dre, who sat staring at the carpet, his gaze fixed and unfocused.

He spoke without looking up, his voice flat and devoid of emotion.

"As soon as I got off the plane, this *monster* attacked," Dre said, his voice tight with emotion. "He slaughtered everyone. Even Dad... he couldn't stop him."

Dre's eyes flashed a vivid purple, fury radiating off him in waves. His fists clenched, muscles taut with restrained power, grief fueling the storm within him.

Bianca, sitting nearby, folded her legs, listening intently. Malachi, hearing Dre's account, felt a cold dread settle in his gut.

The brutal efficiency, the sheer savagery... it mirrored the attack Brooks had unleashed. The same terrifying power, the same ruthless disregard for life.

Ms. Shaka looked up, her voice breaking as she said, "Why? One tragedy after another—I just can't take it anymore," and tears started to fall. As she said this, she whispered, barely audible, "Lord, take this case... and give me the pillow." Bianca immediately reached out, wrapping her in a comforting hug.

Watching his mother cry, Malachi felt a sharp twist in his chest. The pain was heavy, a physical weight.

He glanced at Dre and Miguel, searching for solace, for some shared understanding.

Miguel, his face etched with exhaustion, ran a hand over his eyes, trying to compose himself.

Dre sat back on the sofa, hands shoved deep in his pockets, the strain of the evening evident in his slumped posture. Suddenly, the television flickered to life, the news reporter's voice cutting through the heavy silence.

"The island is in ruins," the reporter stated grimly, "with an estimated fifty thousand lives lost tonight. This is being deemed a national disaster..."

Bianca gasped, covering her mouth with her hand.

"Oh my goodness," she whispered, her voice choked with horror. Miguel, without a word, reached for the remote under him and switched off the television. "My bad, guys," he mumbled, the apology barely audible.

Silence descended again, heavier now, thick with the weight of the news.

Malachi glared down at his sister, his grief and anger a silent storm raging within him.

He was struggling, processing the enormity of the loss, the devastation. The weight of it pressed down, a physical burden he could barely bear. Then, Ms. Shaka's voice, soft but firm, broke through the oppressive silence.

"Perhaps we should pray," she said, her words a fragile lifeline in the churning sea of his despair.

But even as she spoke, a different kind of storm was brewing. The wind whipped across the sun-baked cliffs of Patmos, carrying the scent of salt and the cries of gulls, a stark counterpoint to the quiet grief.

Vultures, perched like macabre gargoyles, stirred restlessly on the jagged peaks surrounding the ancient seal – a silent witness to the impending chaos.

The seal itself, a massive pillar of obsidian rock amidst swirling storms, split open with a deafening roar that echoed across the Aegean Sea, mirroring the shattering of his world.

Dust, glimmering with the ethereal glow of moonlight, billowed outward as fissures spread across its surface like spiderwebs, a visual manifestation of the unseen cracks in his soul.

From the heart of the shattered seal, figures emerged, their forms grotesque and terrifying.

First emerged a figure, his face a skull-like mask with blue glowing irises. He wore a bloodied, ripped old west outfit, enhancing his eerie presence.

He crouched low to the ground, his massive hands scooping up a handful of sand, his guttural breaths rattling like stones in a cavern.

Beside him stood a woman of ethereal beauty. Her pale skin glowed in the sunlight, pink hair cascading down her back. She wore revealing green armor, and her sharp pink eyes scanned the landscape with a predatory gleam.

Behind them, a parade of horrors emerged from the shattered prison.

A towering figure loomed, with brown skin and straight hair contrasting with beastly features. Blackened lips revealed sharp fangs, while fiery red eyes burned beneath bushy eyebrows, and a claw-like beard adorned his chin. Sniffing the air, he rumbled, "Our masters are here."

Trailing behind him was a grotesque, vibrant blue figure, fat and lumbering, with two horns. Around his neck hung a black necklace featuring a twisted emblem—two lines with a circled smile. "What a wonderful era to be reawakened," he mused, eyes gleaming. "Humans are plentiful; it's a feast—"

A pink-haired girl interrupted with a swift backhand, shattering his jaw. Black blood oozed, but it quickly regenerated. He chuckled darkly. "You're lucky you're my sister," he warned. "Try that again, and you'll be my next meal."

Clad in dark red armor with a shadowy cape billowing behind him, he advanced confidently from the shadows. A massive sword strapped to his back and a polished helm concealed his face, yet his aura radiated power and cruelty. As he emerged, he cast a scornful gaze upon the others.

The skull-faced one shouted, "Silence, you plague!" as he let the sand slip through his fingers, rising to stand defiantly.

A bandaged figure in a white cloak emerged, one purple eye visible. He leaned weakly against the cracked opening of the pillar, shielding his face from the sun.

A child with smoke-gray skin, white curly hair, and pale eyes emerged from the pillar, patting him gently. In a soft, childlike voice, the child said, "It's okay, we are free now."

The hulking, bone-masked figure, his voice a gravelly rasp, spoke first, "Our masters were here." The skull-faced one glanced at him, then directed his gaze outward, scanning the horizon with a sense of foreboding.

Locking eyes with the frightened human, the skull-faced one narrowed his gaze with calculated menace and declared, "Scatter, little prey. Run while you can, for the hunt is upon you."

The pink-haired girl, her voice a melodious counterpoint to the bone-masked figure's harshness, chuckled, a sound both beautiful and chilling. "What a time to be alive," she purred, her pink eyes gleaming with excitement.

The blue figure turned to her, staring in astonishment, clearly mind-blown that she echoed his own earlier words.

The bandaged figure, with a low, languid voice, nodded. "Indeed," he murmured. "This ignorant world will be... *fun* to end." Beside him, the child chuckled softly.

To be continued...

CHAPTER 22- THE CALVARY

A week had passed since that fateful night, but for Malachi, time blurred, each day haunted by memories of battle. In the quiet of his bathroom, the absence of his eye forced him to rely on other senses, sharpening his perception of a world now changed.

Easing into the porcelain tub, pain mingled with flashes of past battles: serpentine creatures, Jermaine's frantic heartbeat, the clash of Noah and Ronaldo, and the moment he saved Alexis. Azazel's shadowy presence lingered, but it was Fabian's absence and Bianca's trusting eyes that truly haunted him.

Determined to grow stronger, Malachi embraced his new routines. In the golden light of day, his promise to protect whispered through the lavish bathroom. "I won't fail again," he vowed, his heart steady with passion.

As he lay in a luxurious bath, sunbeams danced across marble tiles while he raised his fist, droplets falling like diamonds.

Malachi gazed at his fist, its knuckles bruised from his last clash with Azazel. The moonlight highlighted the calluses, each a testament to arduous training. "I won't fail again," he murmured, a vow carried on the night's breeze.

Azazel's haunting words echoed: "They're not just damaging; they're disintegrating me at a molecular level."

With a shiver, Malachi flexed his hand. Was there something extraordinary about his punches? Could they truly cause such destruction? This realization was both frightening and exhilarating—a power beyond mere strength.

Determined to understand and control it, Malachi knew the path was perilous. Yet, he yearned to harness this power fully, to protect those he loved and ensure he never failed again.

The cemetery's green expanse, dotted with solemn headstones, stood as a testament to lives lost. Clad in black, Malachi and his companions gathered, their grief hidden behind shades, each silently promising to find strength for those they had loved and lost.

Malachi's voice, heavy with regret, pierced the afternoon stillness. "If money could buy happiness, I'd pay any price to bring them back."

Bathed in golden sunlight, he grew silent, recalling Vance's playful assurance: "When my time comes, don't cry for me. I'm saving spots in heaven for you and Miguel." The memory lingered, a poignant mix of sorrow and enduring hope.

Bianca, her gaze tender on Vance's headstone, whispered, "I think about him often. Even as an outsider, he treated me like family. I can't bear losing you guys."

Miguel smiled warmly, "We're here, Bianca. Not going anywhere." He slung an arm over Dre's shoulder, lifting his spirits, and added, "With Dre back, we're unstoppable."

Jermaine knelt by Fabian's tombstone, reminiscing about the love shown by Vance, "He showed more love in one night than I've known. Fab… he was the light." Ronaldo added, "Literally."

Their words honored bonds that transcended loss. As Alexis walked by, she thanked Malachi and Ronaldo. Miguel introduced himself and began flirting, leaving Alexis intrigued. Captivated by their conversation, they soon drifted away together.

Before leaving, Malachi whispered "Rest in heaven, Uncle" at Vance's grave and fist-bumped Fabian's stone. After quick bro hugs with Dre, Jermaine, and Ronaldo, he told Noah, "We'll talk." As they walked away, Malachi tapped Dre, who lost in thought, looked up and said, "Yeah, yeah."

Hand in hand, Malachi and Bianca stepped into a new chapter together. As they left, he heard the guys say he was lucky. Noah added, "He's just blessed."

His nerves were apparent as he admitted, "I like you, too," making her blush.

Their moment was interrupted by Deon and Peter's approach. Peter, in a trench coat, his arm around Deon, brought with him memories Malachi wished to forget, fears unspoken yet vividly alive.

Malachi and Bianca paused under a tree. Bianca glanced over at Dre, who seemed withdrawn. "Is Dre alright?" she asked softly. Malachi nodded, but she gently pressed, "And how about you?"

He sighed deeply, "I feel like I should have done more to save them."
Bianca gently rested her hand on his arm, her touch a soothing balm. "You did everything you could. No one could have foreseen what happened."

Gathering her courage, she confessed, "Even with everything spinning out of control, I have to tell you—I have feelings for you, and I think it's mutual."

Malachi looked at her, surprised but intrigued. "What makes you so sure?" he asked with a teasing smile.

Her eyes sparkled. "Because of the way you reacted. Don't play with my heart. But if you're ready, I'd love to start something real with you."

Malachi's heart swelled, and despite the teasing words that came to mind, he simply said, "I'd love that, too."

Bianca let out a joyful laugh, quickly covering her mouth as she giggled. Malachi joined in, drawn to her warmth. "What was that?" he grinned, pulling her into a tender embrace.

As they embraced, Malachi's eye trailed Peter and Deon descending the hill, a shadow crossing his heart. Dre, sensing a sudden chill, instinctively looked back at Malachi, drawn by an inexplicable shift in the atmosphere surrounding them.

The JDF base hummed with a low thrum of anticipation, as rows of recruits sat rigidly in the large briefing room, a sea of expectant faces.

Malachi and Miguel burst through the double doors, late as usual. Malachi shot Miguel a withering look. "You almost got us kicked out," he hissed, his voice low but sharp.

Dre, sitting near the back, didn't glance up. A jagged scar bisected his nose, another slashed down his right eye, a grim testament to past battles. Jermaine and Noah sat beside him, their expressions grim but resolute. "You guys here?" Malachi asked, his tone softening slightly.

Jermaine grinned, a flash of white teeth against his dark skin. "Somebody's gotta share your pain, man." He bumped fists with Malachi, who nodded to Noah in acknowledgment. Miguel, hands shoved deep in his pockets, leaned toward Dre. "How you holding up, Dre?"

Dre's eyes, dark and hollow, met theirs. He looked like he hadn't slept in days. A curt nod was his only response. "You boys good?" he asked, his voice a gravelly whisper.

"Never better," Malachi replied, a hint of bravado in his tone.

On the small stage, four figures stood silhouetted against the bright lights. Captain Mark's commanding presence was beside Renée, her blonde pixie cut a striking complement to his stern demeanor.

Next to them stood Cornrow, a nuclear specialist whose black shirt couldn't quite conceal the network of scars that crisscrossed his arms, and an older man in a sharp black suit, his head shaved clean.

Renée, her voice amplified by the room's sound system, welcomed everyone to the JDF.

"How's everyone feeling?" she asked with authority, the room buzzing with nervous energy and excitement.

"This," she continued, gesturing to the assembled recruits, "is the largest intake we've had in years." She turned to Captain Mark, a question in her gaze. He simply stared back, his expression unreadable. Renée sighed, then turned back to the crowd.

Miguel muttered to Malachi, "She seems... different."

"Mhmm," Malachi agreed, his gaze fixed on Captain Mark.

Captain Mark stepped forward, his voice cutting through the murmur. "Before we begin," he said, sweeping his gaze across the recruits, "I want to know if you understand what the JDF stands for. What is our motto?"

A murmur rippled through the room. Miguel mumbled, "Justice, Duty, Fortitude."

Renée's eyebrows shot up in surprise. "Right, Miguel," she said, amused. Miguel looked startled that she'd heard him.

Captain Mark, one hand casually in his pocket, continued. "The JDF—Jamaica's Defense Force—is our last line of defense.

Our goal is simple: to protect society from all forms of evil. We're talking everything from rogue Awakened individuals to malevolent spirits—and yes, demons.

The majority of you here today were directly involved in the catastrophic attack on our island; it triggered your powers.

We keep the regular humans safe and sound from everything that goes bump in the night. Think of us as... soul reapers but with a lot more paperwork." He paused, letting his words sink in. He then looked directly at Malachi, Miguel, Jermaine, and Noah.

With a resolute yet encouraging voice, he addressed them, "You four have been chosen to embark on this journey with my squad." His eyes met theirs, filled with determination and belief.

"Welcome to The Cavalry, where each of you will discover your true potential, and together, we will rise to any challenge."

As Captain Mark finished, the rest of the captains stepped forward, each calling recruits with purpose.

One by one, names echoed through the room, tying destinies together with every squad formed. Each team gathered around their respective leaders, faces a mix of determination and trepidation.

The weight of their new roles settling on shoulders too young yet too battle-hardened for their age, they prepared to stand as protectors against the darkness.

To be continued...

CHAPTER 22- NOT JUST LUCK

The two-week journey to Goat Island was a blur of travel, punctuated only by brief rests and snatched meals.

They arrived to find an island consumed by an endless, dense forest; a primordial green expanse that seemed to swallow the light. The air hung heavy with the scent of damp earth and decaying vegetation.

Back on the mainland, during their downtime, Malachi and Miguel found themselves immersed in ancient texts on Spiritual Energy, their frustration simmering beneath the surface. Miguel, in particular, chafed under the academic approach. One evening, after a particularly intense study session, Malachi exploded.

"This is ridiculous!" he roared, slamming his book shut. "We didn't join the JDF to read dusty old books! We signed up to save humanity, remember?"

Mark watched from a distance for a moment, then calmly walked over. The argument between them was heating up, but luckily it hadn't turned physical.

"Alright, enough," Mark interjected with a firm tone, locking eyes with both of them. "Let's get something straight: you were both targeted. And as for you," he added, turning to the one with the scarred eye, "that wasn't just bad luck."

And Miguel," he gestured to Miguel's arm, a solidified mass of molten rock, "that's not just a burn. We're dealing with something far beyond your comprehension."

He paused, letting the gravity of his words sink in. "I have high hopes for you both.

I expect you to be at the top of your game. But the behavior of these evil spirits... it's unpredictable and erratic. That's why we're here, on Goat Island. To train. How long? That depends entirely on you."

Their training on Goat Island focused on harnessing Spiritual Energy. Mark taught them to sense Spiritual Energy signatures through their senses – Miguel learned to smell it, Malachi to feel it – and to enhance their bodies with it.

He explained the basics: how to draw upon it, how to channel it, and how to use it to augment their strength, speed, and reflexes.

Finally, they disembarked from the boat onto the island's shore. The air hung thick with the smell of damp earth and decaying vegetation. Miguel surveyed the oppressive jungle, a frown etching itself onto his face.

Malachi observed the surroundings, his expression serious. "This better be worth it," he said, his voice low.

"Because this place looks like it's going to try and kill us slowly."

Mark tossed them their backpacks with a smile. "Ever think about how our ancestors not only survived but thrived in places like these? They turned challenges into wins, and we can too.

"Mark then effortlessly jumped from the boat onto the muddy bank. He landed with a light thud, the movement fluid, and practiced.

Mark walked over to greet the scientists with a chuckle. Among the group was a Black woman with braided hair and circular glasses, her eyes full of curiosity and wisdom.

Miguel flung his backpack onto his back and patted Malachi on his back. "At least we don't have to put up with any goats here on Goat Island!"

Malachi rolled his eye and shoved him. "That's not even funny, dude."

Miguel chuckled, undeterred, as they continued on their way.

As they reached the group, Mark said, "Oh, Cindy, these are Enoch's sons, Malachi and Miguel." Cindy warmly shook their hands. "Oh, royalty," she said with a smile. Miguel's eyebrows shot up, clearly impressed.

Cindy, always curious, asked, "So, what brings you guys here?" Malachi thought, "She ain't even know we were coming."

To add to the suspense, Cindy pulled out a tablet, grinning, "I hope this isn't one of your secret operations, Mark."

Mark chuckled and replied, "Oh, nothing too secretive... I'm just here to train these two." He added with a wink, "If you don't tell anyone, I won't either. Besides, this is for the island's good, and these guys have serious potential."

He spoke with the confidence of someone who trained their uncle Aron.

The brothers were surprised to hear Mark mention that he had trained Uncle Aron. After all, Uncle Aron was the third strongest in their clan, and it was pretty impressive that Mark had been the one to train him.

Cindy tapped her pencil, a playful smile on her face. "Discretion is appreciated, but secrets are irresistible," she said, raising an eyebrow.

"Just keep those two out of trouble!" She turned to a Chinese scientist, speaking rapidly in Mandarin.

The others headed for the lab. Mark asked what that was about. Cindy replied, "The JDF sent a mysterious compound. They can't identify it, but it triggers awakenings."

Mark whistled. "Well, I'll be damned. So someone's jumping the gun, skipping the natural order?"

Cindy looked around. "This is classified," she said, her voice low. "But the higher-ups are trying to cover this up. Why? I don't know. That's why a captain like you hasn't heard about it."

Mark opened his mouth to ask Cindy more about the mysterious compound, but she cut him off.

"Ain't you got training to do, Captain?" she said, a playful smirk tugging at her lips. He paused, a chuckle rumbling in his chest. "Alright, alright. Boys, follow me. Lab tours next, then we'll get down to business."

Cindy, her back to them, was absorbed in her tablet. He stopped, turning back. "I beg your pardon?" He repeated himself, his voice firm. Cindy finally looked up, her expression serious.

"That's not happening," She pointed over to a clearing. "Whatever training you're doing, make sure it's over there. This whole area is under tight surveillance."

Moments later, they stood in a wide-open training yard bathed in afternoon sun. Mark, a formidable figure, dominated the space.

His dark, sleeveless vest hung loosely over a worn linen shirt, his dreadlocks neatly braided into a ponytail, and his bushy mustache and beard added to his imposing presence.

In contrast, Miguel and Malachi, in simple shorts, appeared almost slight, their youthful energy a stark contrast to Mark's seasoned strength.

After three weeks, Malachi's eye still had faint claw marks. His other eye was intense, with the white turned black and a mid-knight blue-crescent iris."

Mark clapped his hands, the sound sharp and resonant. "Alright, gentlemen. Let's see what you've got. No holding back."

Miguel grinned, his eyes flaring with an inner fire, a fiery orange glow illuminating his pupils.

"Sparring with the guy who robbed us of our Freedom? This is gonna be legendary!" Malachi mirrored his enthusiasm, a wide, confident grin splitting his face. His gaze, however, flickered between his scarred eye and

Mark, a hint of apprehension underlying his bravado.

"Tell you what," Mark said, a glint in his eye. "I'll hold back. You boys go all out."

Malachi and Miguel exchanged a quick fist bump, then assumed fighting stances, their bodies coiled with anticipation.

 Miguel moved first, a blur of motion. He spun his legs a whirlwind of kicks, each strike accompanied by a burst of flame. Mark, however, was a wall of controlled power, effortlessly sidestepping the fiery attacks.

Spotting an opening, Malachi raced around a tree and appeared behind Mark, aiming a punch at his back. Mark reacted instantly, a backkick sending Miguel sprawling, his fist intercepting Malachi's blow with a sharp *crack* that sent a jolt through the air.

"Good strategy, Malachi," Mark said, his voice low. "Poor execution." Malachi, undeterred, grabbed Mark's arm, attempting to throw him.

Mark pulled his hand away, quickly spun Malachi by the shoulder, and landed a heavy punch right into his chest.

The hit was so hard that Malachi coughed up blood, with the sickening sound of cracking bones filling the air. Before Malachi could even react, Mark delivered another strong punch straight to his face.

Malachi slammed into the boulder with a force that cracked it, the sharp pain in his chest making him wince. He sat there, breath ragged, blood trickling from his nose and mouth, leaving a crimson trail down his chin as he tried to catch his breath.

Miguel's eyes went wide. "Whoa, that was brutal!" he muttered, caught between awe and worry for Malachi. He just stood there, unsure of what to do next.

Miguel clapped his hands, fists igniting with blue flames. Growling, "My turn," as he charged forward.

Mark met Miguel head-on, landing hook after hook, pushing him back through the area. He grabbed Miguel, slamming him into a tree before flashing forward with a double-fist strike. Blood spilled from Miguel's mouth, but he gritted his teeth as he slid down.

Mark massaged his knuckles, glancing between the boys who were both a bloody mess. "Okay, what did we learn here?" he asked, his tone stern but concerned. "You rushed in without thinking.

You've got to be more strategic. And remember, we're enlightened humans, not immortal. Your lives are valuable.

He urged them to practice using soul resonance to heal their injuries, emphasizing its importance for their survival. He warned sternly that if they didn't improve, he would keep breaking bones repeatedly until they mastered it.

With a pointed comment, he added, "By the time I'm finished with you, using soul resonance will feel as natural as breathing."

To be continued...

CHAPTER 23- M.O.G

Five days later, Mark wandered through the forest, the quiet broken by rustling leaves. He smiled, spotting signs of someone nearby—a bit of disturbed moss, a snapped twig.

He stopped, hand raised as if signaling a halt, a knowing smile spreading across his face before he smoothly spun on his heel.

Just then, Malachi leaped from a tree branch, Mark cackling. Malachi punched the air with precision, and Mark instinctively shielded his face as the force rushed toward him.

The force of Malachi's punch shattered the trees around him, splinters slicing through the air and dust billowing up from the ground.

Miguel launched himself from the cover, his hands a blur as he unleashed a wave of intensely blue flames. The air crackled with ozone as the cold, searing tendrils shot toward Mark, leaving a shimmering trail of sapphire light.

In a sudden turn of events, Mark unexpectedly appeared between them, one stick aimed at the back of Malachi's head and another poised at Miguel's throat, turning the encounter into a tense standoff.

He dropped the sticks with a laugh. "Just messing with you guys!" he exclaimed, clapping his hands. "Seriously, you've both improved immensely. Anyone else would be toast. You two make a fantastic team."

Miguel shook his head with a grin. "Damn it, we almost got him!" Meanwhile, Malachi turned to Mark, curiosity piqued.

"What are your powers, anyway?" he asked.

Mark smirked. "That's your homework, guys. Figure it out."

He winked; a breathtaking flash of emerald briefly swirled within his eyes before fading back to their usual brown.

Malachi chuckled, "Bet."

They found a secluded spot by the river, the gentle rush of water a soothing counterpoint to their earlier intensity. Mark cooked salted fish and roasted breadfruit over a small fire, and they ate from banana leaves. Between bites, Miguel asked, "Hey Mark, why the JDF?"

Before turning serious, Mark grinned, "Truth be told, it was a dare. Lost a bet with your old man.

 Couldn't let him have all the fun, could I?" He shared stories of his past – escapades and humorous mishaps – laughter punctuating the meal.

They weren't just sparring partners anymore; they were becoming a close-knit unit. Malachi, chewing thoughtfully, leaned forward. "So, what's the real reason you're training us?"

Mark leaned back, the playful glint in his eyes fading. "I've always been a bit of a rebel, never fitting in with the system. I've seen how the superhuman world works, and frankly, it's broken.

"I'm starting with you guys as my pupils," he said excitedly. "Together, we'll build a world where super-humans can stand up for themselves and others, free from control."

He smiled at them. "You are the beginning of this new era."

Mark sipped from his coconut, with the sound of the nearby spring in the air. Right there, in the forest, it felt like the start of something special.

Mark got up and smiled, saying, "Alright, we've crushed phase one. Let's jump into phase two." Malachi, finishing off his coconut, raised an eyebrow and asked, "So, what's phase two all about?"

Mark laughed, "That's where we get creative and work on developing new attacks." He paused, looking around at the group. "I just want to let you all know how proud I am. You've done an incredible job so far."

With a ripple of displaced air, Mark vanished.

Miguel's eyes widened. "He can teleport!"

Malachi shook his head. "I don't think so."

"Then what? Super speed?"

"I don't know," Malachi admitted, "but it's not either of those."

"Negro you slow," Miguel teased.

"Malachi looked over and said, "Shut up, Golem," Miguel, trying to hide his rock arm behind him, just replied, "Wow."

In just hours, Miguel unleashed his fiery potential. Mastering Inferno Weaving, he shaped flames into walls, nets, and a thermal blade. His pyrokinesis let him control fire effortlessly, while Spiritual Energy control refined his attacks.

He forged fire constructs and discovered fiery wings for flight. With heat manipulation and flame throw capabilities, he projected intense blasts and Spiritual enhancements boosted his strength and resilience.

Miguel became a powerful blend of fire and Spiritual Energy, ready for any challenge.

Malachi, however, struggled with his Spiritual Energy training. His attempts resulted in erratic bursts and uncontrolled flares.

It was during one of these frustrating sessions that he noticed Li Wei, a sharp-minded scientist with quiet confidence, observing him from the edge of the clearing.

Curiosity piqued, he approached her. The fiery sword Miguel had conjured earlier provided a striking visual contrast to the image of the controlled, focused energy Malachi hoped to achieve. He felt a renewed determination to master his powers.

"Why so far from the lab?" he asked.

"Even the brightest need fresh air," she replied with a grin. "Out here, energy feels different—real."

Recognizing Malachi's potential, Li Wei helped refine his abilities with her insights and advanced technology.

Under Li Wei's watchful eye, Malachi's journey of transformation unfolded. Sunlight played through the paper screens, illuminating his path of growth and mastery.

Every morning began with meditation, an introspective exercise that unlocked Malachi's spiritual energy. Beads of sweat hinted at his progress as he fortified his body, achieving a resilience that mirrored steel.

His spirit blade wasn't merely a weapon; it pulsed with life, becoming an extension of his innermost resolve and precision. Each swing was a testament to his strengthening bond with this elemental force.

Under the tutelage of Li Wei, Malachi pushed beyond his physical limits, embracing newfound strength and agility. He moved with a fluidity that seemed innate, a dance woven with the grace and power of a warrior.

In playful revenge, Malachi lay in wait at the waterfall and, spotting Miguel, he punched a shockwave at Miguel with a mischievous grin.

Their laughter echoed until they froze—Mark had returned, his shock evident. Their Spiritual presence had grown so powerful that they rippled across the Caribbean, reaching a city in Florida.

Mark's final duel with them underscored their growth; he won.

Under Mark's relentless guidance, Malachi and Miguel underwent a grueling training regimen that pushed them to their limits. Despite Malachi's frequent complaints, they were driven by the demanding schedule.

They practiced intense meditation to master energy control, engaged in high-intensity workouts to build endurance, and refined their skills with energy-infused weapons.

Nature training grounded them, while study and mental challenges enhanced their understanding and resilience. Even their dreams became arenas for overcoming barriers.

Through it all, Mark's unwavering focus transformed them, complaints fading as they emerged stronger and spiritually empowered.

Malachi splashed his face with water at the spring and suddenly found himself standing on a shimmering surface that sparkled like liquid sunlight. Overcome with joy, he stomped the water beneath him, marveling at the surrounding grand buildings with their gleaming columns and intricate carvings.

The air, filled with a sweet floral scent, wrapped him in serenity, each breath refreshing in the tranquil atmosphere. Only the gentle lapping of water against nearby pools broke the silence.

His left eye, wide with wonder, took in the breathtaking scene, though the slashed scar on his face stood in stark contrast. The lush and peaceful vision invited him to explore, blurring the line between dream and reality.

He heard a calm voice call his name. Turning, he saw a man with long white hair and fiery eyes. The man gave off a warm glow, saying, "How are you doing?" and hugged him, making Malachi feel like they'd known each other forever.

Gently touching Malachi's scarred eye, the man said they'd met before. When Malachi asked if he was an Awakened, the man invited Malachi for a walk.

As they strolled, Malachi confessed his fears, worried about facing Azazel again

and letting others down. The man assured him, "You're not alone."
The man told Malachi, "Just have faith in the Almighty."

Malachi confessed, "I feel like the Almighty wants nothing to do with me and is disappointed in everything I do." The man placed a comforting arm on Malachi's shoulder.

The man spoke with gentle encouragement. "You may feel lost now, but the Almighty hasn't turned away from you. Trust in your path and yourself. You're doing everything you're supposed to be doing, even if it doesn't feel that way."

He said, "You were called to deliver a message, not to doubt. Remember when I said you'd do greater work than me?" With that, he encouraged Malachi, "Go and be the man you were meant to be."

Suddenly, Malachi found himself back in the spring. Li Wei walked up to him, clearly excited.

Li Wei said, "Malachi, you're something special. Your skills are revealing new sides of Spiritual Energy, and it's pretty unpredictable.

"Listen," she said, her excitement palpable. "Both your spiritual energy and your lunar powers are evolving. Normally, if someone relies too heavily on one aspect, it can take over their essence. But in your case, your lunar energy is growing stronger."

He raised an eyebrow, skepticism etched on his face. "What do you mean?"

She leaned in, her voice animated. "I think it's because you're suppressing it. When you hold back, that energy builds up—like a pressure cooker. Once you absorb enough lunar energy, it's going to reach a critical threshold and combust!

The potential for a massive release is incredible, but you need to be careful. If you don't channel it properly, it could overwhelm you!"

He sighed, frustration still evident. "Great, just what I need—more pressure."

She gasped, a look of realization crossing her face. She touched his arm excitedly and exclaimed, "Guess what? We've made a month's worth of progress! Isn't that awesome?"

Malachi blinked in surprise. "A month? What do you mean? We've only been here for two weeks."

Li Wei chuckled, clearly amused. "You didn't know? Mark can speed up time!"

The realization hit Malachi just as Mark and Miguel arrived, urging them to move quickly. Before they left, Li Wei handed Malachi an eye patch that resembled a headband, intricately designed with subtle patterns. "Come back anytime," he said with a grin, a twinkle of mischief in her eyes.

Malachi thanked her and asked for his name.

"Li Wei," she replied.

Malachi joined his friends, the ocean breeze welcoming them back to reality.

To be continued...

CHAPTER 24- SECRETS

The boat glided smoothly into the dock, releasing Miguel and Malachi onto the sunlit pier. They were greeted by Mark's steady presence and reassuring nod. "Take today to relax," he advised, his voice thoughtful and authoritative. "We'll gather our thoughts and meet tomorrow."

"Thanks, Mark," Miguel replied, his voice sincere.

Malachi hesitated momentarily, grappling with his words before speaking. "Your guidance has been invaluable."

Their conversation was interrupted by the arrival of an imposing black and gold limousine that purred to a stop nearby. Its opulence was impossible to ignore. "Who's that?" Miguel questioned, a hint of skepticism lacing his words.

Mark's expression shifted to one of gravity. "Have you heard of the Ancestor Shore Council? They're the hidden force that shapes the island. Exercise caution."

"I am Theron. I represent the Ancestor Shore Council. The elders require the immediate presence of the twins. Your attendance is not merely requested; it is mandatory." His gaze swept over them, assessing, calculating.

"And if we refuse?" Miguel inquired, his tone steady but probing.

Mark turned his gaze to meet theirs, his eyes conveying the weight of the decision. "I strongly suggest you hear them out. This could be pivotal."

Seeing the mix of determination and urgency in both Mark's demeanor and the envoy's approach, Malachi nodded in agreement. "All right. Let's see what this is all about."

With a shared sense of resolve, the twins moved toward the limousine. The weight of the moment hung heavily in the air, hinting at the mysterious events about to unfold on this enigmatic island.

As they were led into the dimly lit meeting room, Miguel and Malachi immediately noticed Dre, Jermaine, and Noah already seated at a long, polished table. Taking a seat, Miguel broke the ice, asking, "Did they get you guys too?"

Malachi grinned, exchanging a fist bump with each of them. Jermaine leaned back in his chair, raising an eyebrow. "Yo, where have you boys been? I swung by your place, and you were gone."

Miguel gave a slight nod, a hint of mystery in his smile. "We were training."

Something caught Malachi's eye—the distinctive logo embroidered on Dre's jacket shoulder. His brows furrowed as he pointed. "What's this?"

Dre hesitated before replying, a touch of pride in his voice. "I was waiting to tell you. I joined the clan. My family drew their last straw, and this was the only way forward."

The right-hand man, who had been quietly observing, pocketed his phone and addressed the room. "Alright, since we're all here..."

Jermaine whispered urgently, "What's this all about?"

Miguel shook his head slightly. "We don't know. But listen, just say what they want to hear. It'll grant you protection from the Shaka clan. But you need to be loyal."

The right-hand man moved to switch on a large TV mounted on the wall. As the screen flickered to life, sound bars appeared, dividing into four sections. The audio that emerged was heavily distorted, shrouding the speakers' identities.

Noah leaned forward, obviously intrigued. "They've taken hidden to another level," he remarked, eyes glued to the screen.

"Pay attention," the right-hand man cautioned. "The elders are about to speak."

"Your victory over Azazel was... impressive," the distorted voice crackled from the screen, a hint of grudging admiration coloring the synthetic tones. "Truly remarkable was the ingenious way you managed to anchor him in one location, enabling us to finally send Azazel back to hell."

A tense silence filled the room, broken only by the hum of old technology. Jermaine shifted uncomfortably as Malachi, seated with his one sharp eye keenly observing, remained still, arms crossed.

"However," the voice continued, the tone shifting subtly, "such rapid growth... it presents... complexities. Opportunities, certainly, but also... challenges to the established order." The words hung in the air, heavy with unspoken warnings.

Another silence, longer this time, pregnant with the weight of unspoken power dynamics. Then, the voice resumed, its tone carefully calibrated to convey both invitation and subtle threat.

"To ensure the island's continued prosperity... and to leverage your considerable talents... we propose a... strategic partnership. A mutually beneficial arrangement, we believe."

Miguel leaned his head to the side, a skeptical look on his face. "Mutually beneficial? Let's hear the specifics. What are the strings attached? And what happens if we refuse?"

Jermaine, oblivious to the tension, blurted out, "So, what's the plan? What do we do?" Miguel shot him a look and subtly mouthed, "Shhh."

The distorted voice, though still carrying a hint of static, sounded less threatening, more... pragmatic. "Let's be frank. Our previous communication was... inadequate.

The partnership we propose isn't easily explained. It involves... access. Access to resources beyond your current comprehension, to knowledge spanning centuries, to opportunities that would reshape your destiny. In return, we require... collaboration.

A certain... alignment of purpose. Think of it as... a necessary exchange. The specifics are... intricate. Suffice it to say, your continued existence, and indeed the future of this island, is inextricably linked to your participation. Refusal... is not an option we can afford to consider."

Miguel's voice, laced with apprehension, was firm. "So, it's not about control, but... necessity? A 'necessary exchange,' you say. Sounds like a hostage situation with extra steps.

This... 'partnership'... what is it exactly? I've never heard of this council, these elders. What happens if we refuse? What are the consequences? What happens if this... 'dam' you speak of... breaks?"

The elders, wise and resolute, addressed the room with urgency. "The world as we know it is shifting. The old order of dominant nations is crumbling, and

Jamaica, once among the top 20, must navigate this change," one elder began.

"In our land, the Big Three clans—Shaka, Somers, and Heart—have long stood as pillars of strength and stability. They have protected us, harnessing the island's ancient energies to maintain balance," another elder continued. "But today, they face a formidable threat, one that respects neither boundaries nor traditions, seeking to exploit our weakened state."

The elders turned to the younger generation. "We need you. Your connection to the island's energies and your innovative thinking are crucial. You are not bound by the past, and with your help, we can rejuvenate the clans and forge alliances beyond traditional hierarchies."

"Our role as elders is to guide, but your role is to lead us into a new era. Together, we can create a society where unity defines strength, securing our future in this changing world. It's time to step forward and shape this new order, honoring our history while embracing the future."

Their message was clear and hopeful, calling on the youth to take up the mantle and lead the transformation.

As they stepped onto the rooftop, Jermaine noticed that the door they had just come through had turned into a solid brick wall. "I should be surprised, but I'm getting used to this," he said with a chuckle.

Miguel grinned. "That's the spiritual awakening for you—makes the bizarre just another Tuesday."

Dre, leaning thoughtfully on the railing, confessed, "I didn't know Jamaica had secret leaders."

Malachi, standing next to him, was watching the construction workers below with a keen eye. "Given Jamaica's power, it's logical. The strongest don't need to be visible to lead."

Noah asked, "So, what should we do?"

Dre, his voice carrying the weight of experience, replied, "Nothing. They stay hidden for a reason. The Big Three clans wield both influence and power. Even one member remaining is enough to keep others at bay."

He hesitated for a moment, then continued, "I left my clan because they were stuck in the old ways and crossed some serious lines. It wasn't easy, but I found a new path with Malachi and Miguel's clan. They're forward-thinking and never blind to change."

Malachi nodded, understanding both what Dre had lost and found. "Our power balance is intentional. It's about knowing where we fit and respecting the past without being shackled by it."

                                        To be continued...

CHAPTER 25- DARK CLOUDS

The twins found their mother serene, a stark contrast to the tension that filled the room moments later. Their playful greeting morphed into a heartfelt reunion as their mother's relief and pride mingled with unshed tears. She voiced her unwavering support for their dangerous path, surprising Malachi with her understanding.

A tender, hurried farewell, punctuated by the jarring sonic boom that rattled the windows, left them breathless.

Malachi adjusted his burgundy jacket, the smooth wool a familiar comfort against the lingering chill. He carefully arranged his locs, ensuring they completely covered his eye patch. Stepping onto the stairs leading down to the lake, he spotted Bianca in the parking lot, chatting with a group of girls.

He paused, considering whether to eavesdrop. His enhanced hearing, a subtle side effect of his... abilities, picked up snippets of their conversation. One girl excitedly boasted about her new job as a nurse.

A group across the lot spotted him. A wave of recognition rippled through them. "Malachi!" one called out. The excited shouts, "Malachi! Oh my god, Malachi!" echoed as the girls rushed towards him, a wave of delighted greetings washing over him.

"You remember us! You got us out of the hotel!" they praised. Malachi, unsure of the memory but warmed by their gratitude, accepted their hero worship with a quiet smile—it felt good to be called a hero.

The girls departed, their excited chatter fading into the distance. Bianca's smile faltered, replaced by a weary expression. She nervously brushed at her arms, a tremor betraying her exhaustion from the day's events.

"Hey," Malachi said, approaching her.

Her eyes brightened. "Hey," she giggled, launching into a hug. "How are you doing?"

They separated. "I'm fine," she said, then added, "You smell amazing."
In the car, a tray of food sat between them in the back seat as a movie played softly from her phone on the dashboard. Bianca took a sip of water, her gaze lingering on Malachi. "I never thought you'd be interested in me," she confessed, her voice barely a whisper.

Malachi, happily forking mac and cheese into his mouth, bumped her playfully. "You know what's funny? From the moment I saw you..." he began, then paused for dramatic effect, "...I knew."

Her eyes widened. "Really?"

He adjusted his dreadlocks, the strands falling neatly in front of his eyepatch.

"I'm so glad we're doing this," she said, her voice firm, a stark contrast to her earlier uncertainty. She launched into a vivid description of their future: her as a therapist, him as a doctor, eight kids... "Eight?" he questioned, eyebrows raised. "Stay with me now," she laughed, her eyes sparkling with mischief.

Malachi told her about joining the J.D.F. The words hung heavy in the air, settling on her like a weight. "I thought the plan was... not to be like your dad," she said softly, her voice laced with concern.

"I know," he said, his voice low and urgent. "But with literal demons coming after humanity, and my family on their hit list... I have no choice."

Bianca's hand instinctively grasped his, her touch grounding him amidst the rising dread.

A cold knot tightened in his stomach. Subtly flexing his fingers, he detected several distinct spiritual presences—a chilling wave of dark energy, the nature of the approaching threat unclear, but undeniably hostile.

"There's always a choice," she countered, but her voice lacked conviction.

Silence fell, punctuated only by the movie's soundtrack. Bianca bumped his shoulder. "You know," she said, a teasing lilt in her voice, "you make wearing an eyepatch look... good."

He bit into a patty and coco bread, crumbs falling onto his shirt.
He turned to her, his eye meeting hers, and softly said, "Don't."

"Sorry," she murmured, grasping his hand.

He grimaced, noting, "mh, your hand is greasy," as he felt the slick texture.

He felt her hand close over his, guiding him to rest over her chest, near her heart. "What...?" he began, his voice barely a whisper, his nervousness palpable. The question died in his throat as he felt the frantic, wild beat of her heart beneath his palm, acutely aware of the proximity of his hand to her breast.

His own heart mirrored the rhythm, a frantic drum against his ribs. Her smile was serene, a beacon in the storm of his anxiety.

"Silence," she murmured, her voice soft but firm. "These scars, they are ours to share. You will never fight alone again. You have God... and God has brought me here, to fight beside you. This is our battle now."

"I know you're hurting," she whispered, "but I'm willing to stand by you till my last breath if you'll have me as your bride."

He smiled, a soft, amused light in his eye. "Shouldn't I be the one saying that?" he teased.

She released a melodic, enchanting laugh. "Oh my goodness, Mal," she said with a playful glint, "I'm not proposing!"

With a playful grin, Malachi set the food tray aside on the driver's seat and settled back down. She leaned in to kiss him, a tender brush of lips that conveyed more than words ever could.

He pulled back for a moment, cupping her face in his hands, and gazed into her eyes, the depths reflecting all his answered prayers.

"I've prayed for moments like this," he confessed softly, "and I want nothing more than to have you by my side." Then he kissed her, pouring all his love and promises into that single, unending moment.

Suddenly, an explosion shattered the serene atmosphere. Malachi instinctively turned, peering through the back windshield. Standing amidst the debris and dust, four figures appeared, motionless and unfazed. They wore black hoodies and menacing carbon skull masks.

At the center stood a lean figure, dressed in black hoodies and cargo pants, a cap crowning his head.

A dark grey carbon fiber skull mask, marked by two bold white lines, hid most of his face, while his fiery, orange eyes blazed with unsettling intensity.

Beside him stood a girl with an exposed midriff, exuding a poised defiance as she held her ground.

Bianca asked with concern, "What is it?" Malachi told her calmly to lock the doors as he stepped out of the car, the door closing with a decisive thud.

Through the window, her anxious eyes followed him while she quickly secured the locks.

Malachi's eye flared with an intense blue glow, the whites turning black. The masked figure, his mask marked by jagged white streaks, addressed them with chilling politeness. "Apologies for the intrusion, but we require the girl."

Malachi couldn't believe it. *They think this is okay out in the open like this?*

"If you don't want to die," he growled, his voice low and dangerous, "I suggest you go back where you came from."

The masked brute beside him scoffed, his mask obscuring any expression. "Who the hell does this guy think he is?"

The masked figure, white streaks slashing down his mask, said in a low voice, "That deadhead over there? He's from one of the Big Three clans.

He stared down a prince of Hell and only lost an eye doing it. I suggest you handle him with extreme caution."

Malachi frowned, wondering how they knew so much. "So, you're the leader?" he asked, his voice dangerously calm.

The guy shrugged casually in response to Malachi. "Something like that," he said, turning to his goons.

"Wish it was just a grab-and-go, but with the dreaded here, we've gotta deal with him. Go at him all at once, but don't kill him," he instructed.

Then he settled himself on a bench, leaning forward with his arms on his knees, hands clasped together, watching the scene unfold.

The brute cracked his knuckles with a grin. "Sometimes you just gotta mix things up a bit," he said.

Meanwhile, Malachi formed his spirit blade, the energy shimmering in his grip.

Watching this, the girl hesitated. "Are we doing this? I'm not so sure about taking him on," she said, uncertainty clear in her voice.

The brute cracked his knuckles with a wicked grin. "C'mon, don't chicken out now. We've got this."

The short goon sprouted six additional arms, projecting an unsettling challenge. Malachi found the transformation grotesque. Nearby, the brute expanded in size, casting an imposing shadow over the scene.

Malachi darted forward with lethal precision, his blade slicing through the air and skillfully severing three of the goon's arms on one side, the dismembered limbs thudding to the ground.

In the instant that followed, the girl unleashed a stream of blood toward him. Malachi spun effortlessly, deflecting it with a flat-handed block, then slipped from his stance to blitz toward her at astonishing speed.

As his blade arced toward the girl, the brute intervened, lunging to intercept. His hand closed around the blade, but he cried out in pain and wrenched it away, the weapon still lodged deep in his shoulder. He groaned as the fearsome burn intensified. Unwavering, Malachi tore off his mask.

The brute instinctively raised his arms to shield his face as Malachi's powerful front kick slammed into him.

The impact sent the brute hurtling backward into the staircase, the stone splintering under his weight with a thundering crash. Dust and debris filled the air, swirling around him as he lay momentarily stunned by the force of the blow.

Malachi gripped his sword firmly, poised to throw. As he did, a wisp of flames erupted nearby, revealing the leader enveloped in a fiery aura. With a swift motion, the leader deflected the oncoming sword using a blade that blazed around his fist, scattering sparks in a dazzling arc through the air.

The leader turned his head slightly, eyes locking on the brute as he struggled to rise. "Gather the others and leave," he commanded with quiet authority. "I'll handle this."

Seriously, I can't trust you guys with anything," he barked at the brute.

"What?" the brute retorted, eyes narrowing.

The leader shot him a sharp glare, voice heavy with a reprimand. "If I hadn't stepped in when I did, you'd be meeting the devil right now."

The leader tilted his head up, peering at Malachi from beneath the brim of his cap. A glimmer of grudging respect flickered in his eyes as he spoke, "Looks like I'll have to deal with you myself."

Malachi's voice was firm as he said, "Do you think that's a good idea?"

The leader shrugged casually and said, "Doesn't matter—you'll be dead soon anyway." He smirked, throwing in a jibe, "Besides, I heard your family isn't much to brag about either."

The leader lunged, hands flickering with flames, thrusting them towards Malachi. Malachi zipped past the fiery attack, grabbed the leader's hood, and slammed him into the ground with a bone-jarring thud.

He brought his foot down for a stomp, but the leader rolled away, narrowly avoiding the blow.

Malachi glared, then saw Bianca cheering wildly, a "Whoop!" escaping her lips. He looked at her, a sheepish grin spreading across his face as he sat down, muttering, "Oops." "Mal, watch out!" Bianca yelled.

Malachi turned just as a wave of searing flames struck his face, leaving angry red welts and a smoking burn across his cheek. He groaned, falling to one knee. The leader crouched beside him, his expression a mixture of anger and sorrow.

"It never had to be this way," the leader rasped, his voice low and strained. "Your family... they caused this.

I'm not going to kill you just because you don't use your family's powers. But... your girl... pray she's strong. Because she definitely won't make it."

As Malachi's facial wounds miraculously healed, he lowered his head and, with surprising force, headbutted the leader.

The leader stumbled back, his forehead bleeding, the face mask he wore crushed and broken. Malachi saw the leader's face for the first time, and the leader, clutching his head, exclaimed, "What the heck, man?!"

A brilliant blue laser-like beam erupted from Malachi's palm, striking the leader full force. The leader was blasted backward, smashing into the railing of a nearby staircase with a sickening crack of splintering wood.

He landed in a heap, his body smoking, his clothes scorched and torn, groaning in pain from the impact and the searing energy.

"Okay, okay, you've got me, bro," he admitted, wincing as he lay there on the staircase, his body smoking, burns marring his skin from head to toe, half his face obscured by scorched flesh. "But just so you know, we're not after you."

Malachi's sword vanished, his single eye narrowing in frustration. This wasn't the resolution he had sought.

The words struck Malachi, instantly turning his thoughts to Bianca. It was clear now—Bianca was their true target, and Malachi knew he had to protect her at all costs.

Malachi spun just in time to see a hooded goon effortlessly toss Bianca over his shoulder. A mocking salute followed, and, without hesitation, Malachi burst forward.

The sheer force of his speed cracked the air, sending a shockwave that rattled nearby cars and scattered dust.

As he closed in, the goon became wrapped in a dark, swirling mist. Malachi reached into the shadows, fingers finding purchase on something solid, and with a strong pull, the mask came free.

Instantly, the mist vanished, leaving the goon's face exposed, eyes blazing with malice.

Around them, the other goons had disappeared like phantoms.

Malachi looked to the bystanders gathered —some whispering, others recording on their phones. Yet Malachi remained unfazed, indifferent to the revelation of his powers. All that mattered was Bianca's safety amidst the unfolding chaos.

To be continued...

CHAPTER 26- SLOW DOWN

Malachi sat in the driver's seat, one leg dangling onto the asphalt, staring at the mask in his lap. He thought of Bianca, of the life they'd planned together. Then two figures approached—Miguel and Dre.

Miguel spread his hands wide and said, "What up? Got your text." As he looked around the wrecked parking lot, he added, "Heck happened here?"

Malachi showed them the mask. "Bozos wearing these masks took Bianca."

Miguel's eyes widened. "What? What do you mean, they t big ook her?"

Malachi replied, his voice tight, "Exactly what I said. They took her. Even though I beat them, they still got her."

Dre, usually laid-back and carefree, let out a low whistle, but the casual air was gone, replaced by a simmering anger. "You gotta be joking."

"I wish I was," Malachi said, running a hand through his hair.

Miguel frowned, confused. "Why would they take her, though?"

Malachi shrugged. "I don't know, bro." The anger in Dre's eyes was palpable now, a stark contrast to his usual easygoing demeanor.

Miguel said, "How'd you even let that happen? Were they demons?"

Malachi looked at him, flabbergasted. "No, they weren't demons! They were four awakened, like us! He chuckled, a nervous sound. "You wanna know what's funny? One of them had fire powers."

Miguel was taken aback. "What? You sure?"

Malachi was shocked by his own words as if the realization was hitting him anew. "Would I lie?"

Dre, his earlier anger still simmering, said, "I thought *you* were the only one with fire powers."

Miguel, trying to lighten the mood, joked, "Could be a long-lost cousin. Or maybe he's another brother. Probably some kind of anomaly, like me."

Malachi leaned back, thoughtful. "We know Dad's been loyal to Mom since forever," he said.

Miguel pondered for a moment before suggesting, "It could be one of our uncles—probably Uncle Eric or Uncle Matthew."

Malachi shook his head, recalling past conversations. "The two you mentioned? Uncle Eric and Uncle Matthew? They can't have kids where they're at."

Just then, Dre's phone chimed. He glanced at the screen and looked up at them. "Speaking of your uncles," he said, showing them the text. "Family's calling a clan meeting."

With urgency in their steps, they moved down the corridor, the path to the meeting room both familiar and foreboding. As they entered, the room framed by four imposing sofas seemed to pulse with an underlying tension and expectancy.

At its heart, seated on the central sofa, was Uncle Aron. He radiated an aura that filled the room with an almost palpable force.

A man of imposing stature, he had curly locks tied in a knot that crowned his head like a warrior from ancient tales.

His attire—a black and gold dashiki suit—draped around him, shimmering with understated elegance, yet there was something almost regal in its simplicity.

The room was heavy with unspoken tension. Miguel approached Uncle Aron, the casual hand clap feeling strangely out of place. "Uncle Aron," he began, his voice lacking its usual playful lilt, "what's up?"

Aron, a mountain of a man in his dashiki, simply grunted in response, his gaze sweeping over the assembled family. The usual boisterous energy was absent, replaced by a grim quietude.

"We got some bad news," Aron finally said, his voice low and gravelly. He didn't need to elaborate; the gravity of his tone spoke volumes.

The news of Gramps's critical condition hung in the air, unspoken but universally understood. Whispers and nervous glances circulated among the assembled family members. Catherine's gasp was barely audible, a choked sob swallowed by the collective anxiety.

Aron continued, his voice hardening slightly, "And it's not just Gramps. The demon attack... we lost people. More than we're letting on." He paused, letting the weight of his words sink in. The casual chatter was replaced by a stunned silence, punctuated only by the occasional sniffle or whispered prayer.

"But that's not all," Aron said, his gaze hardening. "There's a bigger threat coming. Something... different. Something we haven't faced before." He looked directly at Malachi and Miguel. "The Seven Deadly Sins."

The brothers exchanged a grim look. The casual joking was long gone, replaced by a shared understanding of the impending danger. A nephew, emboldened by the shared fear, asked, "What are they?"

Aron explained, his voice devoid of its earlier casualness. "Sixty years ago, they manifested. They wreaked havoc. Gramps and others sealed them away. Now... they're back." His frustration was barely contained. "That's why we need everyone here. We're all in this together."

Malachi, his face grim, spoke up. "I have something to add. Bianca's been kidnapped."

A collective groan went through the room. Aron's disappointment was palpable. "I'm sorry, Jr., but we can't spare anyone. Not even for this. The JDF will have to handle it. We need every available person to prepare for the Sins."

Malachi's jaw tightened. He knew the JDF's limitations. He nodded curtly, "I understand." He turned to leave, the weight of his loss and the impending battle heavy on his shoulders.

Philip, one of the triplets, blurted out, "Mally, don't go doing nothin' stupid now."
The comment ignited a powder keg. Malachi turned, his eye blazing. "That's supposed to mean what, exactly?" Philip, oblivious to the danger he'd just invited, grinned. "You know... like father, like son."

Malachi's spiritual energy surged like an unstoppable force, pushing everything back as if an earthquake had erupted in the room. His cousins frantically conjured shimmering barriers, their voices urgent as they called for him to calm down, fearing he might lose control in his mounting intensity.

Malachi, his voice dangerously low, said, "Repeat that. I'm positive I didn't hear you." Philip, terrified, curled up on the sofa, begging, "Please, I'm sorry! I didn't mean it!"
Miguel shouted Malachi's name, trying to de-escalate the situation. Aron, his voice strained, pleaded, "Jr., calm down! You know he's not the brightest bulb in the box!"

Catherine rushed to Malachi's side, her voice tight with apology. "Malachi, I'm so sorry. Philip's stupid, he doesn't know any better. Please, forgive him for me. I'm begging you." The energy subsided, but the tension remained thick.

Malachi glanced aside a barely perceptible twitch of his lips, then sucked his teeth.

With a crack of displaced air, a ripple of heat, and the earth trembling faintly beneath their feet, he vanished in a sonic boom, leaving a stunned silence and a lingering smell of ozone in his wake.

Miguel followed instantly, leaving a faint afterimage of motion.

Dre, his face a mixture of guilt and concern, mumbled an apology to Aron. As he passed Philip, he gave him a death stare. Aron, his face etched with weariness, simply sighed.

Catherine, however, was furious. She rounded on Philip, her voice low and dangerous, "What is wrong with you? Malachi is hurting, and you make it worse? You need to learn some respect."

Deon, putting a comforting hand on Aron's shoulder, added quietly, "Malachi already hates my dad, and I get the brunt of it. Next time, try to be better."

The elevator hummed softly as Malachi descended, tension thick despite the modern setting. He leaned against the wall, mind racing, while the warden beside him recited rules he eventually tuned out.

With a jolt, the elevator stopped, doors opening to a high-tech containment cell.

Inside, a glass cube housed essentials: a bed, a toilet, a sink, and a table. Confined to a metal chair with shackles on his feet and his hands imprisoned within a metal box, his uncle nevertheless wore a knowing grin, framed by his dreadlocks. A case glowing with high-tech purple lights sat beside him.

"My man! The red line! You gotta remember, don't cross it! Don't!" the warden cried, his voice bordering on hysteria.

"My boy," his uncle began, the words barely a breath. His pure blue eyes, usually warm and kind, now held a chilling intensity as they fixed on the eye patch. A long silence stretched between them, broken only by the deadly whisper that finally escaped his lips: "Who... do I have to kill?"

A hand went to his eye patch, a fleeting touch. "Mh," Malachi breathed, the single sound carrying a weight of finality. "The one who did it," he stated, "is already in hell."

His uncle chuckled. "Well, I'll be," he said, the implication clear. "I thought *I* was the bad seed in the family."

"Not quite," Malachi answered. "Heard of Azazel?"

"Only from the Book of Enoch."

"Yeah, he did this," Malachi revealed.

Impressed, his uncle asked, "Did you beat him?"

"You could say that."

His uncle laughed. "So, what brings you here? I thought I said no more visits, remember?"

Malachi's tongue clicked a sharp, frustrated sound. He felt utterly lost. A demonic attack had stolen his eye, leaving him scarred and vulnerable.

Vance was dead, and whispers of foul play surrounded his father's death, adding to the growing sense of dread. Bianca's kidnapping, happening immediately after their kiss, was a wound that refused to heal. Aron, instead of offering support, had coldly instructed him to wait, leaving Malachi feeling abandoned by his own family.

The looming threat of the Seven Deadly Sins only amplified his despair. He watched his mother and Miguel crumble under the weight of grief, their pain a stark contrast to the hollowness that had settled within him.

The inability to comfort them, to ease their suffering, was a torment that cut deeper than any physical wound. His anger burned, a fierce, impotent flame against the overwhelming darkness that threatened to consume them all.

Uncle Eric closed his eyes, his lips pressing into a thin line. When he opened them again, the usual twinkle was gone, replaced by a hard, knowing glint. He didn't offer empty platitudes; there were no assurances that everything would be alright. Instead, he spoke plainly, the words blunt but laced with a gruff kind of empathy. "Life ain't a fairy tale,

Malachi," he said, his voice low. "We all got our trials, our tribulations. You're going through yours, and there ain't no magic fix." He paused, watching Malachi's reaction. "Talk to God, boy. Pray. Pray for your mom and Miguel. But you can't save them right now. You gotta save yourself first."

Malachi mumbled something about praying but receiving no answers. Eric cut him off, his voice firm. "You ain't giving Him a chance, son. You gotta be patient. Wait. Let Him work."

Malachi, desperate for guidance, finally asked the question that had been burning in his gut. "What do I do about Bianca?"

Eric considered this, his gaze distant for a moment before focusing again on Malachi. "Find her," he said, his voice firm but not unkind. "Do everything you can. But remember, sometimes, the hardest battles aren't fought with fists, but with faith and with your wits. Use both. And don't forget to pray for her, too."

To be continued...

CHAPTER 26- THE NIGHT

Malachi, deep in the city's underbelly, pursued a shadowy organization responsible for unleashing "enlightened" death row inmates and abducting children. He'd rescued two recruits, but a bullet grazed his shoulder, and the weight of accidentally killing an inmate pressed heavily on him. Exhausted and wounded, he continued his relentless pursuit.

Meanwhile, Miguel, driven by worry and brotherly loyalty, tracked Malachi's path. He found his brother beneath a city bridge, weary and burdened by his mission. Their reunion was short-lived; a terrifying oni-like creature attacked.

A brutal fight ensued. Malachi and Miguel fought valiantly, but the creature proved resilient. Just as they were overwhelmed, Jermaine and Noah arrived, adding their considerable skills to the fray. The battle raged, the creature displaying unnerving strength and resilience. Finally, Mark arrived, wielding a small, well-worn book.

It wasn't magic, nor an energy weapon, but a book functioning like a highly advanced, focused spiritual weapon—a kind of "spiritual bible," its contents acting as a conduit to banish evil spirits and demons.

With a precise reading of specific passages and a fervent recitation, he weakened and ultimately banished the creature. The brothers were bruised but alive, the immediate danger gone, but the larger conflict, and the loss of their friend Bianca, still loomed large.

For Malachi, the victory felt more spiritual than technological, leading to a profound awakening. He realized the deeper implications of their struggle against darkness and the importance of hope, fueling his resolve to fight for those suffering in the shadows.

Entering the house, Malachi's mom rushed over, hugging him tightly. Pulling back, she cupped his face, concern evident in her eyes. "What's wrong with you? Oh, God," she said, her voice trembling. She glanced at Mark and whispered, "Thank you."

Mark nodded and turned to the twins. "We'll talk more tomorrow," he said before leaving.

Ms. Shaka faced Malachi, her voice rising. "Malachi! Why didn't you—" Tears welled in her eyes. Miguel stepped in, wrapping his arms around her. "We love you, Malachi," she said, her voice cracking.

"I know, Mom," he replied softly, guilt creeping in.

"Let her finish," Miguel urged.

Ms. Shaka gripped their shoulders. "I left my family because they wanted to change me. But seeing you two grow fills me with pride. I love you both."

At that moment, Malia appeared, rubbing her eyes. "Mommy?"

She gasped and ran to Malachi, who scooped her up, smiling. "You missed me?"

"Yeah!" she exclaimed.

Ms. Shaka smiled but turned serious. "Your family loves you. Please don't do this again. And I know Bianca's alright."

Malachi's smile faded. "Yeah, but..." Doubts creased his brow, while Miguel stood nearby, slipping into a shadow of sadness.

"Mom," Malachi whispered, "I don't want to let you down."

She pulled him close. "You could never let me down. Remember, we're in this together."

That night, Malachi lay in bed, using his hands as a pillow, thoughts swirling in his mind. Demons wanting humanity's souls, the evil spirit declaring it wouldn't let them have what was meant for them, the Syndicate, Bianca, and the spiritual encounter on Goat Island. He rubbed a hand over his face, muttering, "This whole thing is a mess."

A knock at the door interrupted his thoughts. "Mal, you sleeping?" Miguel's voice called from the other side.

"Nah," Malachi replied.

Miguel entered and shut the door behind him. Malachi sat up, and Miguel settled next to him. "Why didn't you come to me, bro? Aren't we brothers? We've been through everything together."

Malachi pushed his locs out of his face, frustration evident. "I wasn't even thinking. My mind was on one thing, and everything else was blank."

Miguel sniffled, glancing down. "Well, since you were after the Syndicate, why didn't you go after Alexis's father?"

Malachi sighed, the weight of the question hanging in the air. "I... I don't know. It just felt too complicated."

Miguel clenched his molten rock arm, chin raised. "I'm kinda glad you didn't," he said.

Malachi looked at him, confused. "Why's that?"

"Because of Alexis," Miguel replied. "We're taking it seriously. She's been through a lot, and she's building a bond with her father. It'll break her if she finds out he's part of a secret organization that kidnaps kids."

"Yeah, you're right," Malachi agreed. "What do you want to do about it?"

"I want to keep it from her," Miguel said firmly.

Malachi frowned. "I don't know, man. I can try to steer things in a different direction."

"That's not what I want," Miguel said, capturing Malachi's full attention. "I want all of this and her dad as far away from her as possible."

Malachi smiled, understanding. He placed a hand on Miguel's shoulder. "I'm sorry about what I put you through the past few days."

Miguel tapped his hand. "You know we're like enemies right now, right?"

"What do you mean?" Malachi asked.

"Your girlfriend got kidnapped by my girlfriend's dad," Miguel said with a chuckle.

"Yeah, but it's way deeper than that. We're more than brothers; nothing's changing that," Malachi reassured him.

"Exactly. Speaking of which, where in the world is Dre?" Miguel asked.

Malachi thought for a moment, realizing he'd forgotten about Dre. "Shoot, I don't know. Ever since he left that meeting, he's been MIA."

"He'll come around when he wants to. You know he's not a people person," Miguel said.

"The man lost his whole family in one night. He needs his friends," Malachi replied.

"I tried reaching out to him, but nothing. We just gotta wait." Miguel covered his nose and mouth, groaning. "Since Dad died, everything just went left."

Malachi shifted the conversation. "Do you know what 'regression to the mean' means?"

Miguel shook his head.

Malachi explained, "It's the idea that things tend to return to their average state over time. After something extreme happens, conditions usually balance out. It's like life pulling back to normal after chaos."

"Makes sense," Miguel said, nodding. "It's like how we pray because we need Christ more than ever."

"Absolutely," Malachi replied.

As they spoke, they performed their signature handshake, gun fingers tapping against each other before they locked their fingers. With a final snap, they separated a shared smile of camaraderie between them.

To be continued...

CHAPTER 27- REFLECTION

In the military room, tension hung thick in the air, the hum of the AC unit a stark contrast to the charged atmosphere. Malachi hunched over a computer, eye glued to the CCTV feed, scanning for threats.

Nearby, Miguel and Jermaine pushed through their workout routine, each movement a display of disciplined focus, embodying the resolve needed for what lay ahead. Noah lounged casually with his phone, while Kyle idly spun a lighter, the flickering flame casting shadows that danced across the walls.

The door swung open, and Mark strode in with a clap, commanding immediate attention. "Alright, boys, listen up."

Malachi remained absorbed in the screen, prompting Miguel to call out, "Mal!"

Frustration etched on Mark's face as he crossed the room and unplugged the computer, breaking Malachi's concentration.

Startled, Malachi snapped his head up, eye narrowing defensively. But Mark's calm demeanor eased his stance. "Group meeting. Now," he said firmly.

Malachi joined the circle, receiving a fist bump from Noah as they gathered. "So, we all know today's the clan meeting," Mark began, his tone serious. Jermaine raised an eyebrow. "It's today?"

Kyle, arms crossed, leaned forward. "So that's why it feels like a storm outside." Malachi glanced out the floor-to-ceiling windows. The sky churned with dark, roiling clouds, though the air remained eerily calm.

"Yeah, but there ain't no storm coming," Mark remarked, his gaze steady. "That's the clan heads' spiritual energy at work."

"Are they really that strong?" Noah asked, skepticism lacing his voice.

"Of course," Miguel replied, conviction in his tone. "They're the ones keeping the nation safe, especially now that the sins are coming."

"Sins?" Jermaine questioned, confusion flickering across his face.

Mark's voice turned grave. "The Seven Deadly are approaching. All those tremors, the destruction in Europe—that's them."

Kyle leaned forward, urgency in his tone. "Are they the embodiment of the sins, or just people claiming to be?"

"They're the true incarnations of sin," Mark stated, his expression hardening. "Born from humanity's darkest deeds."

Jermaine, shaken, crossed himself, and murmured, "Christ, we need you."

Noah counted on his fingers, bewildered. "So, we've got the Seven Deadly Sins coming, the Syndicate's schemes and these fallen angels attacking. What's going on?"

"Don't forget about the evil spirits," Malachi interjected, his voice steady.

"They've been getting smarter," Kyle noted, nodding gravely. "We've got our plates full."

"Were they always this powerful?" Miguel asked, concern creeping into his voice.

"Oh no," Mark replied, frustration rising. "They were at the bottom, and now they're getting stronger. They can go blow for blow with us, which never happened before. Their attacks are more frequent, and thankfully, they're only targeting the enlightened ones."

Mark's fists clenched. "We've had fifty-nine reported attacks, and it's pissing me off. I don't get why they're provoking us."

Malachi interjected, recalling their last encounter. "The one that attacked us said something about not letting us get what they were denied."

Miguel nodded, his expression darkening. "Yeah, it sounded like some world domination scheme."

Mark scowled, determination hardening his features. "Exactly. They declared war on us the moment I arrived."

Just then, Dre stumbled through the door, bloodied and dressed in a sleek black tactical jacket with white seams. A white cap contrasted with his attire, and a fitted white vest peeked beneath. His cargo pants tapered into heavy-duty combat boots that thudded against the floor.

In his hand, he held a sword in a sleek scabbard, its curved blade hinted at within. The hilt, partially visible, featured an intricately wrapped grip and a subtle guard.

Miguel was the first to spot him, throwing his hands up dramatically. Rushing forward with concern etched across his face, he exclaimed, "Dre! We've been worried sick. Where have you been?"

Dre's mask covered the lower half of his face, enhancing his enigmatic presence. "Captain," he said, turning to Mark. "You want to break the news, or should I?"

Mark ran a hand through his already disheveled hair. Leaning back, he said, "Look, keep this quiet. Dre's been doing solo shadow ops. He's arguably our strongest Awakened, maybe the strongest among the younger generation, but that kind of power comes with a hefty price tag." The unspoken threat of loss hung heavy in the air.

The room buzzed with disbelief and concern. Miguel's eyes widened, and Jermaine frowned deeply. Malachi, who had always believed himself to be the strongest after surviving his battle with Azazel, blinked in surprise at Dre's presence, remaining silent and resolute. Jermaine raised an eyebrow, skepticism written all over his face. "You can just do that? He's not even part of our squad!"

Miguel shook his head, frustration spilling over. "That doesn't make it okay! We're supposed to operate as a team!"

Mark, steady and firm, replied, "I understand, but we needed someone who could fly under the radar. Dre was the best choice for these discrete missions. It was strategic, not a matter of trust."

Dre walked closer to Malachi and handed him an envelope. "I found this and wanted to give it to you first," he said, his expression earnest.

Malachi opened the envelope and froze, his heart racing as he read the address: an abandoned hospital. Covering his mouth, he pointed at the paper, then looked at Dre. "Wait—this is the Syndicate's hideout?" he asked, disbelief flooding his voice.

Dre leaned on the desk, nodding urgently. "Yeah. We need to move now. They're onto us."

Malachi, his eye filled with determination, told Dre, "I don't know how I'll ever repay you." Dre replied with a reassuring smile, "You don't need to. We ride together, and if it comes to it, we'll face the end together."

Miguel interjected with a chuckle, "Yeah, not too sure about the dying part." Their shared laughter brought a moment of levity amidst their serious mission.

They fist-bumped, the camaraderie sparking a renewed sense of purpose in the room.

Dre turned to the group, urgency creeping into his tone. "We have to move now. I messed up back there."

Mark quickly devised a plan, his voice steady and assured. "Kyle and I will clear a path by dealing with the evil spirits. The rest of you head for the raid."

Miguel hesitated, voicing his concerns. "Five of us against all of them? Is that wise?"

Mark, composed, asked Miguel, "Are you questioning your abilities? Your clan excels at this."

Meanwhile, Malachi called Catherine and Deon for backup. When asked about his relationship with Deon, he simply replied, "Time will tell," before sharing the address.

Mark pulled Malachi into a side room, all serious.

"Malachi, you've been carrying a heavy burden. What your uncle did was wrong, and it's okay to feel the way you do.

But that pain, that fear... it doesn't have to define you. Your power is a part of you, but it's not all of you. You are stronger than the trauma he inflicted. You are in control.

You decide when and how to use your abilities. Start small, find your rhythm, and remember: you deserve to feel safe and empowered."

"No. I don't know if I can. I'm not sure I'm strong enough."

Mark stepped closer, his voice firm but caring. "Malachi, listen. That darkness isn't you. It's a weapon. A seriously powerful weapon. All that anger, that pain... use it.

Don't let them win by breaking you, too. Remember this, youth: Power isn't about dominance; it's about protection. And true strength isn't about crushing your enemies, it's about protecting what you love."

Malachi was silent, wrestling with himself. He pictured Bianca, then the nightmare of what happened. He knew Mark was right, but the fear was overwhelming.

Mark softened his tone but kept his intensity. "Your powers are just that— powers. They're nothing until you give them meaning. It's all about what you do with them, your intention.

Tonight, you decide who you are. You decide how strong you are."

Malachi took a deep breath. "I'll... I'll try," he said, his voice shaky. He wasn't sure, but a spark of determination flickered in his eye—a spark fueled by love and a burning need for revenge.

Mark nodded a hint of a smile playing on his lips. "Well, you've got your orders, Private," he said firmly, then patted Malachi's shoulder. Malachi straightened, a newfound confidence in his bearing, and stepped out of the office to join the others.

As they gathered, they looked to him for reassurance. He merely nodded, standing quietly by the window and pressing a palm against it. Noah broke the silence eagerly, "So, what's the plan?"

Miguel cut in confidently, "With a squad like ours, we don't need a plan. We get Bianca and get out." Jermaine reminded him with a smirk, "You were pretty scared a few minutes ago."

Meanwhile, though the moon was hidden by clouds, Malachi could feel its pulse. Unconsciously, he uttered, "I can feel it." The group fell silent. Miguel, puzzled, asked, "Feel what?"

Malachi replied, "The moon. I can feel it." Miguel moved closer, intrigued. "So, are you using it?"

Malachi nodded solemnly. "Got no choice. I want her back, so I've got to use every ounce of power I have."

To be continued

CHAPTER 28- Y MURDER

The abandoned hospital loomed ominously, its once-vibrant facade now a dull, weathered gray, marked by peeling paint and creeping vines. The building's imposing architecture, with its arched windows and faded medical insignia, hinted at a time when it was a beacon of care, now overshadowed by years of neglect.

Cracked concrete and wild grasses sprouted through the pavement, creating a stark contrast against the remnants of a once-bustling entrance. Surrounding the structure, a narrow alley lined with overflowing dumpsters added to the air of decay, while tangled wires hung precariously overhead.

The damp air was thick with the smell of mildew and rust, mingling with the distant echoes of forgotten voices and the haunting memories of the past. A creeping mist rolled through the area, casting an unsettling chill that wrapped around everything.

Catherine and Deon stood at the entrance, their faces resolute under the flickering glow of a battered neon sign, ready to confront whatever horrors lay ahead within the derelict walls.

Miguel broke the tension with a loud "Yurr!" earning a playful slap from Malachi. Rubbing his head with a faux "Aw," he got everyone's attention. Catherine hugged Malachi warmly, "Hey, Mal," and he nodded, "Hey, how are you doing?"

The group exchanged greetings, their camaraderie cutting through the tension. Catherine's exuberant greeting to Dre briefly lifted the night's heavy mood.

Noah broke the momentary silence. "How long have you guys been here?"

"About fifteen minutes," Catherine replied, her brow furrowed. "It's crawling with Awakened's. They seem powerful—like Stage Fours."

Miguel stretched, cracking his neck with a spark of confidence in his eyes. "Don't worry, we can handle them."

Malachi rested the back of his hand on Miguel's shoulder, his expression serious. "Remember, our sole objective is to rescue Bianca and get out. That's all."

Deon added, "We also need to find out what they're up to and why they're kidnapping kids."

Catherine, with determined nods, organized the group. "Jermaine, Miguel, Malachi, and Dre, take the side route. The rest follow me. We meet back here post-mission." She then instructed Noah firmly, "Guard this spot; no one unauthorized gets in or out." Noah responded without hesitation, "No problem."

With a fist bump, they split off, adrenaline coursing through their veins.

Walking side by side, Miguel and Jermaine chatted easily, the conversation drifting naturally to their abilities. "Hey, how's your firepower holding up these days?" Jermaine asked with a playful grin, flexing his arms to emphasize his point.

"Pretty solid," Miguel replied, nodding in approval. Jermaine chuckled, adding, "Yeah, my Beast Shift's been roaring lately. Feels like I'm getting stronger every day."

The four of them reached the chained twin metal doors on the side of the hospital.

Malachi's hand reached into the night sky, fingers weaving through the silvery strands of moonlight that coiled around them. The threads wrapped tighter, forming a luminous shield that pulsed with quiet, steady energy.

As he stood there, a shadow flickered across his face, a momentary hesitation, like the echo of a painful memory.

His brow furrowed, but With a sharp inhale, Malachi overcame his doubt.

Malachi looked up at the waning crescent moon, which hung like a cold, vigilant eye against the inky sky, casting long, skeletal shadows over the abandoned hospital. The sight intensified his inner conflict as if the moon itself echoed the turmoil within him.

Its light, usually a source of power for Malachi, now felt like a weight pressing down on him, a constant reminder of the cost.

The blue energy coursing across his skin was a haunting reminder of past trauma. As Malachi absorbed it, he felt both determined and apprehensive.

Miguel's urgency pierced through Malachi's hesitation, compelling him to act. When Miguel asked if he was certain it was all right to use his powers, Malachi confessed he wasn't sure.

Yet, the burden of inaction felt far heavier than the pain his abilities might bring.

They stood before a rusted metal door, its paint peeling like sunburnt skin, the air thick with the smell of decay and dust.

He gripped the heavy chains securing it, the cold metal a stark contrast to the burning sensation spreading through his veins. He closed his eye, bracing himself for the tidal wave of memories that would crash over him.

He focused on the chains, channeling the raw energy into his hands. The metal vibrated, then snapped with a sickening crack, the sound echoing through the cavernous, silent halls of the abandoned hospital.

The doors swung inward, revealing four Syndicate goons. The flickering fluorescent lights above cast an eerie glow on their faces, highlighting the grim determination in their eyes.

One, sharply dressed in a black suit, stood apart, his expression cold and calculating. He nodded subtly to the others, confirming their target: "The one-eyed dreadhead."

The sterile white walls of the hospital seemed to amplify the tension, the silence broken only by the ragged breaths of the men.

Malachi released the shimmering dust, a cascade of iridescent particles that did more than dazzle. Each fragment carried a disruptive charge, distorting reality and clouding his adversaries' perceptions with its unsettling presence.

As the dust settled around them, the goons found their limbs heavy and sluggish, weighed down by an invisible force. Panic spread across their faces as they exchanged frantic glances, struggling to move with the eerie weight dragging them into a slow-motion dread.

It was a mesmerizing nebula of particles, sharp with ozone, yet for Malachi, each bit was a shard of trauma, tinged with the phantom scent of blood.

The goons, disoriented by the sudden change in gravity and the dazzling dust, stumbled. Malachi moved like a phantom through the slowed-down chaos.

Malachi moved swiftly, delivering precise strikes among the peeling paint and scattered debris. A kick felled one goon near a gurney, and an elbow dispatched another by a bloodstained table.

As he navigated the chaos, their efforts to form a plan faltered, overwhelmed by the immediate urgency, while he pushed past lingering memories, driven by unyielding focus.

He pinned the sharp-dressed man against a crumbling wall, his forearm a vise around the man's throat.

The man's eyes bulged, his face turning purple. The dust began to dissipate, the gravitational pull lessening. The man coughed, his voice raspy. "You... you found us. You know..."

Malachi tightened his grip, barely registering the man's fear. He was lost in the swirling vortex of his memories, the present a hazy blur against the stark reality of his past. "I know," he said, his voice low and dangerous.

"What was that?" the man stammered, wide-eyed.

"I'm asking the questions," Malachi replied, his voice low and dangerous as he pressed the man against the crumbling wall.

The man swallowed hard. "Well, you found us, so I'm guessing you figured it out."

Malachi yelled, "Of course I know! I was *there*! Now tell me what I need to know before I start breaking bones!"

The man said, "It wasn't us. It was the Vessels who killed your father. We just... supplied them."

"What did you just say?" Miguel's sharp voice cut through the tension, the gravity of the man's words heavy in the air.

"Oh, you meant the girl?" the man responded with a sudden bravado, attempting to shift his stance. With a dismissive smirk, he shoved Malachi back, trying to regain control over the fraught situation.

Dre, seizing the moment, swung his sword, but the man deftly dodged the slash.

He then attempted to shoulder-check Jermaine, but Jermaine remained unyielding, unmoved by the attack.

Capitalizing on the chaos, Miguel let out a fierce yell and delivered a powerful kick. The impact sent the man crashing into the wall, the force reverberating through the confined space of the hallway.

The man sat up, brushing off his clothes, and winced. "Ouch! I'd stay to tangle with you boys, but I've got obligations."

The moment he removed his glove and pressed his palm to the earth, the ground beneath him disintegrated into dust. He plummeted into the chasm that yawned open beneath his feet.

The squad rushed to the edge, anxiously peering into the darkness that had swallowed him, below lay the dimly lit hospital basement, its walls lined with rusted pipes and flickering lights. Shadows danced ominously, and the air was thick with the scent of mildew and decay.

Dre held Malachi back, urgency in his voice. "Find B. I'll go after him." He searched Malachi's eye, sensing the inner conflict. After a moment of hesitation, Malachi nodded, determination settling into his expression.

Jermaine's voice, deep and resonant, cut through the tension. "Mal," he called out. Malachi turned, meeting Jermaine's steady gaze as he nodded toward a door at the far end of the hallway.

"I'm picking up a scent," Jermaine continued. "Down that way."

Miguel, ever eager to move things along, chimed in. "Then that's where we're going."

Malachi, momentarily lost in his brooding thoughts, felt a firm pat on his shoulder. Miguel passed him, offering a knowing smile. "Come on, man," he encouraged, shaking Malachi from his reverie.

Jermaine stared in disbelief. "Your father was murdered? Oh, my word..." Malachi, face clouded, muttered, "I don't want to talk about it," recalling the guard's apology for failing to save his father.

Everything suddenly made sense. Nearby, Miguel's expression was shadowed with murderous intent.

They stepped into a spacious, eerily silent waiting room, the metallic tang in the air mingling with an acrid scent. Jermaine caught a whiff of it first—a thick smoke that curled around them, bringing with it the unmistakable heat of flames.

A roaring explosion erupted, a wall of fire and smoke engulfing them. Intense heat and deafening sound forced them back, their faces illuminated by the inferno's harsh light.

Jermaine reacted instantly, shoving Malachi hard against the wall as the flames roared towards them.

He positioned himself as a shield, a low growl rumbling in his chest, the searing heat making his skin smolder. He held firm, protecting Malachi from the fiery onslaught. Even as the heat intensified, red patterns glowed faintly beneath his jacket on his chest, Jermaine seemingly unaffected by the inferno.

Meanwhile, Miguel spun deftly to the side, avoiding the scorching heat. He quickly aimed his gun-like fingers at the figure behind the receptionist's table. Blue flames swirled around his extended pinky and index fingers, coalescing into a pulsating orb of energy.

Behind the receptionist's desk stood a striking young woman. Her vibrant, golden-blonde hair cascaded in thick curls. Fiery orange eyes glowed from beneath a sleek, black tactical mask.

She wore a cropped black top and a stylish black leather jacket with subtle tactical details, showcasing a toned midriff.

"Forgive me," Aisha whispered, trembling slightly. "They were watching... the lodge... always watching. You should have knocked. They nearly got me." Her gaze was fixed on Malachi.

To be continued...

CHAPTER 29- WHERE THERE IS SMOKE THERE IS FIRE

She moved with a predatory grace. The receptionist's desk cracked and blackened before her, the wood scorching and charring as she effortlessly passed through, leaving a trail of smoking ruin.

"Malachi!" she shrieked a breathless, ecstatic sound. Her hands clapped her thighs in frantic glee.

"Seriously," she said, the smirk barely visible beneath her mask, "that Dark Knight phase? Brooding, mysterious... you were practically a gothic caricature."

"I was *obsessed*!" she giggled, a sound both breathless and calculating. "You were... my masterpiece." She crossed her hands over her heart, her gaze lifting to the ceiling.

She paused, stepping over the wreckage, the smoke curling around her like a shroud.

"But seriously," she snarled, her knuckles white. "Your family... I want to burn their world to the ground. I want to feel the ashes on my skin."

She took a deep breath, trying to calm the waves of anger radiating from her. "Ugh, they're the absolute worst."

Jermaine snorted, nudging Malachi with a teasing grin. "Looks like someone's got a secret admirer, huh?"

Malachi's eye burned with a simmering fury. "Tell us," he growled, the words raw with barely contained violence, "and maybe, just maybe, you'll see the sun rise again."

Miguel rolled his eyes, a sneer twisting his lips. "Yeah, right. Like that's going to work." He hurled a blue fireball, the searing heat washing over her.

A casual flick of her wrist deflected the blast; she barely registered the impact. Then came the roar, the pressure wave, and the sickening crunch of shattering materials. Dust and debris rained down, obscuring the hallway in a cloud of white.

A sharp intake of breath escaped her lips as she recoiled from the pain, her hand already red and blistered. Then, a torrent of furious words erupted. "Miguel!" she screamed, her voice raw with agony and disbelief. "Are you crazy?"

Smoke swirled around them, thick and stifling, echoing her inner turmoil. The silence between her outbursts was even more chilling.

Three goons hurried down the hallway, panic etched on their faces. "Oh dang, it's them!" one gasped. Another leveled a gun, his hand trembling slightly.

The girl's voice was a lethal whisper, devoid of emotion. "If that gun fires, you'll be wishing you'd never been born." Her gaze locked onto the gunman, cold and unwavering.

He approached slowly, trying to appear calm, but the tremor in his voice betrayed his fear. "Aisha," he said, his eyes darting around the scene, "Are you alright? We should... we should probably get you some medical attention."

Her eyes, wild and feverish, lingered on them for a moment. "I'll kill you," she stated the words a low growl. Then, with a terrifyingly calm demeanor, she turned back to the trio. "Prepare to move. Immediately."

Defying physics, they became streaks of motion, impossible blurs, vanishing before the eye could fully register their movement.
Malachi's call to Jermaine was cut short by a low, rumbling growl, a sound both animalistic and supremely confident. "Way ahead of you," Jermaine said, the words barely audible over the sudden burst of speed that carried him after the others.

"Now what?" Miguel asked, tense.

Aisha landed on Malachi, pinning his arms. "Oh hey Malachi, I'm Aisha," she said brightly. "Love the eye patch! Smile more, you'd be a heartthrob."

Miguel's eyes widened. He grabbed Aisha, but his movement was hesitant, almost stunned. He threw her—a reflexive action, not entirely angry. She backflipped, landing perfectly.

Miguel helped Malachi to his feet, eyebrows shooting up in surprise. "Wait, what? Do You love me?

And you're threatening to beat me up?" He chuckled, shaking his head in disbelief. "We just met, and I already feel like I've missed a chapter here!"

A flicker of pain crossed Aisha's eyes before she charged forward, smoke swirling ominously around her. As Malachi briefly choked on the smoke, She dashed toward them with swift precision, enveloping Malachi in a sudden embrace that transitioned into a powerful dropkick aimed at Miguel.

The force of the impact sent Miguel sliding back through the door from which they had entered. In a fluid continuation, she slammed Malachi into the ground with tremendous force, the impact sending cracks spidering out across the floor.

Standing confidently, she pressed a foot on his chest. "I know you're nervous," she teased, "but I'll be bold and ask you out."

His response was cold. "I'm not interested," he replied, swiftly knocking her off balance. As she fell, he caught her by the throat.

Suspended in the air, she struggled to breathe, her eyes turning red. Rising to his feet, he demanded, "Where is the girl with the pink dreads? I won't ask again." She tapped his hand desperately, gasping, "I can't breathe."

He let her drop, and she gasped for air, pulling off her mask. Malachi noted her striking resemblance to Miguel. Miguel entered, stopping short when he saw her.

"You look like me," he said, bewildered. "Why?"

Regaining her breath, Aisha replaced her mask. "You're ugly," she retorted with youthful defiance. "Don't ever say that again."

As she stood, flames flickered in Miguel's palm. "Get up slowly," he instructed. "Alright, alright," she replied, rising carefully.

"Where is the girl with the pink dreads?" Malachi demanded while Miguel asked, "Why is the syndicate kidnapping children?"

She glanced between them, incredulous. "Really? That's what you want to know?" Malachi summoned a spirit blade, its tip threateningly close to her throat.

"Okay," she relented, looking at Miguel. "We're saving them from becoming child soldiers, like us. And I want to live with my brother... and destroy your family.

 But I, really like you, Malachi." She added the last part with a mischievous grin, her eyes sparkling with a mixture of defiance and affection.

Miguel frowned in confusion. "What does that mean?" he asked, holding Aisha's gaze as her cryptic words lingered.

Aisha's expression shifted swiftly from playful defiance to cold fury. In an instant, she summoned a thick, purple smoke that crackled with energy, enveloping the space and blinding them.

As the smoke cleared, Aisha vanished, silence settling in her wake. Suddenly, a chilling whisper came from behind.

"Go away!" she hissed, her voice dangerously low. "You're ruining my date!"

"Date?" Miguel echoed, bewildered. Malachi chimed in, "Yeah, it's a long story."

Vanishing into smoke, she reappeared silently behind them. Miguel spun, unleashing blue flames that crackled through the air.

With a confident gesture, she extended her hands, smoke curling around her fingers. The flames twisted into the haze, their heat diffused as the smoke shielded her effortlessly, rendering the fiery attack harmless.

Malachi struck her with an open palm, the force sending her crashing against the column next to the door.

Her body hit the unforgiving surface, and a sharp, piercing crack echoed through the room.

She froze, her face a mask of shock and pain as Miguel hurried closer.

She coughed, blood bubbling up at her lips, vivid scarlet staining her pale skin as she struggled to breathe.

Malachi took in the grim scene. A broken-off pipe jutted from the wall, its sharp edges glistening with blood, as it rammed through her back and out her chest, marking a horrific path.

Through labored breaths, she remarked on the cruel irony. "I told Ronnie to fix this before it hurt someone. And now, look at me—dying from it. Cliché, right?" she giggled weakly, the sound punctuated by a wet gurgle as blood trickled from the corners of her mask.

Malachi stepped closer, eye wide with regret. "I didn't mean for this to happen," he stammered.

With surprising strength, she placed a fist gently on his chest. "Don't feel bad," she said, her voice steady. "I was no saint. Besides, I had plans to kill your family," she admitted with an eerie calm. "It was us who orchestrated your father's death, made it look like a suicide."

She paused a hint of warmth in her eyes. "Because I respect you, I'll tell you where to find the girl with the pink dreads. She's in one of the surgery rooms on the west side."

A soft sigh escaped her lips. "At least I get to die in front of the two best men God ever created," she murmured, her eyes slowly closing.

As life slipped away from her, Malachi pressed his lips into a thin line. Miguel tapped his shoulder gently, his voice low. "Take it easy. It wasn't your fault."

Malachi nodded stiffly, though doubt lingered. "Sure felt like it," he replied quietly.

Miguel's voice sliced through the silence, suggesting, "She even told you not to feel bad. On the bright side, she's free from this messed-up world now."

Malachi murmured a contemplative "mhmm," the recent events weighing heavily on his mind. Together, they walked down the sterile, dimly lit hospital corridor, shadows flickering as they moved forward, determined yet haunted.

To be continued.

CHAPTER 30- TALK THE TRUTH

With a ferocious burst of blue flames, Miguel blasted a syndicate goon through the twin doors, the charred wood splintering under the force.

As the smoke cleared, the twins stepped through in unison, their silhouettes framed by the flickering azure light. Miguel hovered his palm, still radiating intense heat, over the fallen adversary. With a smirk, he quipped, "Looks like you're fired."

Amid the lingering chaos, Miguel glanced around, his chest heaving with the exertion of battle. "Seriously, how many of these guys do we have to fry?" he exclaimed, the edge of frustration sharpening his voice.

Just then, a heavy, oppressive stench enveloped them, as if the air itself had turned rancid. Instinctively, both men covered their noses and mouths, their eyes watering against the noxious assault. "What on earth is that smell?" Malachi gasped, recoiling slightly.

Miguel feigned an exaggerated gag, and then his gaze caught on something down the hallway. "Check it out!" he pointed, barely managing to suppress a grimace.

Malachi followed his brother's gesture, and his gaze landed on a sign that read "Morgue." A crease formed on his brow, apprehension flickering in his eye. Miguel, ever the one to lighten the mood, remarked dryly, "Why does an abandoned hospital morgue smell like it's still in use?"

They exchanged a tense look. Malachi murmured, "Let's go take a look," just as a deafening explosion thundered above. The building trembled, dust raining down from the ceiling. Miguel glanced up, smirking grimly, "Looks like everybody's putting in work."

Malachi pushed the door open, and it was eerily quiet inside. The morgue was empty, except for the rows of body bags lined up on the floor. Right in the center was a state-of-the-art furnace, its glow impossible to ignore.

His spiritual energy surged like a storm, causing the lights to flicker frantically. The floor beneath them cracked, forming intricate webs across the concrete, and the walls seemed to groan under unseen pressure.

Next to him, Malachi's energy flared with elemental fury. Flames trailed from his eyes, casting a wavering heat that distorted the air. He took a deep breath, calming himself until the fire within cooled to a gentle warmth.

Miguel placed a calming hand on Malachi's shoulder, saying, "Easy now. We'll check it out. If she's here, we'll burn it down together. First, let's look at the body bags, okay?"

Malachi nodded, his voice barely above a whisper, "And if it's the kids..."

Standing in front of the furnace, Miguel turned to Malachi and said, "Hey, it's the kids, bro."

Standing in the doorway, Malachi pressed his lips together, anger simmering. With a deep yell, he swung his fist, smashing the wall into rubble. Yet, the furnace kept burning, reminding them of the horrors inside.

Malachi stood rigid, his fists clenched tightly at his sides, as the weight of the world pressed against his shoulders. "When will this nightmare end?" he murmured, his voice tinged with frustration and weariness.

Miguel, caught off guard by the intensity of Malachi's outburst, turned to him with a puzzled expression. "What do you mean?"

Malachi's eye blazed as he met Miguel's gaze, a torrent of emotions swirling within. "First, we lost Dad, and then demons came.

Malachi, his voice tinged with both frustration and bewilderment, said, "And let's not forget about these vessels. We're clueless about how many there are or even who they are."

And now, there's some secret organization killing kids. When does it ever stop? We're just nineteen, bro! We should be worrying about college, not fighting shadowy groups."

As Malachi voiced his frustrations, a quiet determination began to settle over him, his stance more resolute. "You know, maybe Mark had a point. This power is mine, and I'll use it however I choose."

Seeing the shift, Miguel's concern deepened, anxiety flitting across his features. "What are you saying?"

"Screw Uncle Peter and everything he's done to me," Malachi declared, defiance lacing his words. "I'm done being his puppet." As he spoke, a soft glow began to emanate from the walls, bathing him in an ethereal lunar light. The energy pulsed with a gentle yet unyielding force, cocooning Malachi, and illuminating the conviction in his heart.

Miguel glanced at the shimmering glow, then back at Malachi, whose resolve seemed more unshakeable than ever. "Let's find B and destroy this place," Malachi ordered, his voice steady and unwavering, as he turned to stride down the hall.

Miguel watched him go, worry etched into his furrowed brow. With a silent plea, he sought divine guidance, hoping for strength and protection as they ventured deeper into the unknown.

The rhythmic thud of their footsteps echoed down the long, sterile hallway. The air hung heavy with the metallic tang of blood and something else... something acrid and unsettling. As they rounded a corner, two figures blocked their path.

One was a hulking brute, easily six-foot-five, with thick, muscular arms and long dreadlocks, the tips bleached a stark white. He wore a bulletproof vest that strained at the seams over his considerable bulk. His Syndicate mask hid most of his face, but his eyes burned with a mixture of anger and fear. Red veins pulsed angrily beneath his skin. The woman beside him was smaller, but equally imposing, dressed in a cream-colored sweatsuit and cap. Her large afro peeked out from under the cap, and she, too, wore a Syndicate mask.

The brute's voice, when he spoke, was a guttural growl. "The heck...?" he snarled, his voice thick with barely contained rage. "Babe, get back!" he yelled at the woman, who flinched, fear evident in her eyes as she backed away.

Miguel, Malachi's companion, spoke. "You know him?" he asked, his voice low and dangerous.

"This one of the bastards that took B..." Malachi began, his voice grim. Suddenly, Miguel's dreadlocks and shoulders erupted in blue flames, his eyes glowing a fiery orange. "Homie did *what*?!" he roared.

Before anyone could react, the wall exploded inward. A goon flew through the air, colliding with the brute. Malachi peered through the hole in the wall and gasped.

Bianca stood there, bathed in light, in a nurse's blue uniform. Her irises glowed gold, golden wings hovered inches from her back, and a semi-golden crown adorned her head. She smiled a radiant, almost ethereal smile.

In a flash, the sound of her wings flapping cut through the air as she reached Malachi, his surprise at her sudden appearance palpable. She enveloped him in a warm embrace, her wings hovering gently behind her like a protective shroud.

She cupped his face, her touch lingering, drinking in the reality of him. "To hold you again," she whispered, her voice choked with emotion, "after all this time... after they said you were gone... it's a miracle."

"I'm not going anywhere," Malachi said, his voice low and steady. He held her hand, squeezing it gently, feeling the warmth of her skin against his.

A blush bloomed on her cheeks as she spotted Miguel; she pulled away, her face glowing with warmth, and playfully ran toward him. Malachi felt happiness swell within him, the reassurance he'd given her echoing back to him.

"Miggy!" she laughed, pulling him into a hug full of unspoken reassurance.

Bianca hugged Miguel tightly. "Glad you're alright, girl," he said, his voice warm. She smiled, "I knew you'd come for me!" Miguel chuckled, "Your boyfriend? He was in full-on Batman mode trying to find you. Seriously, the guy was dedicated." Bianca laughed, "I'm glad to see you, too!"

Malachi noticed a faint light beside Bianca, forming into a massive, winged figure. Its dark armor emitted a pure light, and an intense gaze pierced Malachi before vanishing.

Malachi, stunned, thought, *What was that?* The vision lingered vividly in his mind.

Bianca clasped Malachi's hand, resting it against her jaw as they exchanged a tender smile. Watching them, Miguel teased, "I see you got wings now. What, you an angel?" his tone light and playful.

Bianca glanced over her shoulders at her wings, puzzled. "I don't know...," she murmured, "I don't even know how it happened." Her eyes shifted to Malachi and then to Miguel.

"They tried to—" she paused, gazing at Malachi for a moment before continuing, "—break me, and then boom—this happened," she said, her voice filled with wonder and disbelief.

A furious yell sliced through the air, capturing the group's attention. Malachi's smile vanished as he spotted the brute, crouched next to the unconscious girl in the cream cap.

A chilling smile stretched across the brute's face. "This," he hissed, his eyes burning with malice, "is as far as you go."

He lunged toward them with terrifying speed.

"Sit down," Miguel commanded, as blue flames exploded from his palm. The intense heat scorched the air, slamming the brute against the wall. As the flames left blistering burns, the brute's screams of agony echoed through the room, mingling with the acrid scent of singed flesh.

Miguel dropped his hand, and blue flames enveloped the brute crouched on all fours.

The brute body was a colossal figure of molten rock, the very essence of the earth's core. Flames licked at his fiery dreadlocks, the air shimmering with heat as streams of lava flowed across his surface. The once-familiar corridor was now a hellish landscape of scorched earth and crimson light.

Miguel whispered, awestruck, "What in the world?" Malachi nodded knowingly. "Yeah, last time I fought him, he turned into a monster." The brute then rose, a menacing grin spreading as he rumbled,

"Aw yeah," his voice was full of challenge and anticipation.

To be continued...

CHAPTER 31- FIGURE IT OUT

Bianca's fury ignited, a white-hot blaze consuming her frustration. With a guttural roar, she shoved Miguel and Malachi aside, the force of her movement sending them stumbling.

Then, a blinding flash of gold. Her form shimmered, resolving into a figure sculpted from pure, incandescent energy. Before the molten brute could even register the shift, she was upon it, a golden blur against the crimson backdrop of its plasma form.

The brute lunged, double hammer fists blurring into arcs of molten rock, aiming to crush her in searing heat. Unyielding, she blocked with her forearms, the impact echoing like a thunderclap. A shockwave rippled through the air, fracturing the stone walls as the corridor trembled under their clash.

The brute glared down at her with a smirk, "Oh, you got your powers now. About time!

"How about we take that off you," he taunted, his voice dripping with challenge and a gleam of menace in his eyes.

With a fierce yell, she unleashed her strength, shoving his arms aside with a force that seemed unstoppable.

The battle was a demolition, each of Bianca's punches and kicks unleashing the force of a collapsing star and sending blood flying from the brute. Her strikes vaporized chunks of his molten form, filling the space with the sharp scent of ozone.

The corridor shook as his rock-casing body crumbled, unable to fight back. Miguel and Malachi shielded their faces from the heat. Watching, Miguel said, "Wow, she's going in!" Malachi just nodded, smiling in admiration.

With each hit, Bianca's voice pierced through the chaos, fueled by her anger. "I'm so over being everyone's stepping stone!" she yelled, her voice filled with raw fury. "Used, abused, treated like I'm nothing! That all changes today! I'm done playing the scared little girl! This... this ends now!"

The ground vibrated with each impact, the very structure of the corridor groaning under the strain.

Finally, with a spinning backkick that seemed to defy gravity, Bianca sent the brute hurtling through the far wall.

The wall exploded in a shower of pulverized stone, revealing a hidden laboratory – a sterile white space filled with bubbling beakers, complex machinery, and scientists frozen in stunned silence, their faces pale with shock as they watched the destruction unfold.

"Color me surprised," Miguel said, stepping through the hole and whistling. Malachi sensed Deon and Catherine's energy and approached Bianca, taking her hand.

She flicked her gaze to him. "Oh, I'm sorry."

"It's alright," he replied, curious about her condition. Before he could ask, she kissed him repeatedly.

Pulling back, she studied him. "You seem different."

"It's been a crazy two weeks," he admitted. "I'm not at my best, but I feel God has been with me."

"I'm glad to hear that," she said, though her expression turned pained as she revealed burn marks on her stomach. "I just want to go home."

"I'll be by your side," Malachi promised. "With the power God gave me, I'll keep you safe."

Her smile returned as they shared a moment, but Malachi's gaze shifted to Miguel, who had both scientists by their collars. "You folks better tell me what you've got going on here!"

Malachi looked at Miguel and said, "How about we see what's going on here, and then we're home free?"

"Okay," Bianca replied, nodding.

They stepped into the hole, carefully stepping over the brute in his human form —bruised and bloody.

Malachi stepped away from Bianca and moved to the table, picking up a jar filled with clear capsules swirling with blue energy. He felt a static charge and turned to Miguel.

"Hey, check this out," he said, holding up the jar.

Miguel squinted at it. "What exactly are we looking at here?"

The scientist with the afro and glasses cleared his throat. "Those are Ascension pills."

"Ascension pills?" Malachi echoed, intrigued.

The female scientist lowered her gaze, avoiding their eyes. The male continued, "They enhance spiritual energy. The essence of a person's soul is used to create them."

Miguel's expression hardened. "So that's why you're exploiting kids?"

"Bryce I swear to God if yo-" the girl started.

"Shh, let the grown-ups talk," Miguel interrupted, annoyance creeping into his voice.

The male scientist interjected, "That's a different matter. They're extracting abilities from newly awakened individuals."

Malachi's brow furrowed. "And that's killing them? You're stealing their souls."

He began to pace, his thoughts racing.

Malachi spotted the drawers and opened one, revealing folders inside. He pulled one out and showed it to Miguel.

"Wait a minute," Miguel said, eyes widening. "Ain't that Li Wei?"

Bruce looked up. "You guys know her?"

"Yeah," Malachi replied. "She helped me with my powers."

Bianca turned to Malachi, intrigued. "How?"

"When we were training, she was there. It was like she could see the future or something. She knew exactly what I needed to do to master my abilities."

"Mhm," Bianca murmured, absorbing the information.

Malachi shifted his focus to Bruce. "I need you to tell me about the Syndicate—who's their leader and what are they after? Also, tell me about the vessels."

Bruce looked nervous. "If I say anything, they'll kill me."

Miguel smirked. "Is that what you're scared of? I can barbecue you right now."

Bruce gulped but continued. "The Syndicate is a secret organization. It's run by a man they call the Architect. All I know is that he's from Germany, but no one has ever met him. He wants Li Wei—"

"For what?" Malachi interrupted.

"To help perfect the pills," the girl chimed in.

"By the way," Bruce mentioned casually, "the fallen angels' vessels—we're working with them, you know—aren't too happy about you closing the gates of hell. They're trying to get them open again."

Miguel scoffed. "That's not happening. They're constantly reinforcing the veil. It's a waste of time even considering it."

Malachi glared at Miguel, a simmering anger in his eye. That much talk could get them both killed.

Bianca asked about the Architect. "What do you know about him?"

"Look, we only know what we hear. The word is he's obsessed with power, and he's got some kind of group forming, but as far as what he's planning... that's beyond us. It's all speculation."

Malachi opened another folder, his frown deepening as he scanned the contents. "The Syndicate is bigger than I thought," he murmured, a knot tightening in his stomach. "London, Paris...and they're moving on America.

Why are they keeping this so meticulously documented? It's almost...too organized." He trailed off, lost in thought.

Just then, an explosion rocked the building, sending a shockwave that shattered the windows into a web of jagged glass. Flames flickered in the distance, casting an ominous orange glow as thick smoke began to seep into the room.

The heat surged toward them, forcing everyone to flinch as debris rained down and alarms blared.

"What was that?" Bianca asked, wide-eyed.

"Nothing Good," Malachi said, scanning the room.

"Maybe it's our mad cousins," Miguel suggested, a grin forming.

Bianca raised an eyebrow. "So you guys didn't come alone?"

"Not at all," Miguel confirmed. "Jermaine, Catherine, Deon... even Noah and Dre."

"Okay, so I'm important," Bianca quipped with a playful smirk, drawing laughter from the group.

Suddenly, a furious torrent of fiery red projectiles tore through the space. Some slammed into the walls, showering them with blazing debris, while others screamed past Malachi, their heat a palpable threat.

A few fireshots grazed Bianca's closed wings, slipping off harmlessly without a trace.

Amidst the chaos, Miguel swiftly shoved Malachi and Bianca aside, raised his palm, and absorbed the fiery onslaught, leaving only a smoldering silence in its wake.

They spotted a guy advancing down the corridor; his hair was styled in tight, golden twists.

His blue jacket hung open, showcasing a wing tattoo that snaked across his neck and a hawk tattoo on his hand. A cigarette smoldered in his fingers as he blew out a plume of smoke.

Fiery red eyes blazed with intensity as they locked onto Malachi, then softened slightly into a predatory grin.

He ground the cigarette under his heel. "You came a long way for your mansion, rich boy," he spat out, the words laced with contempt.

Bianca stared at him with malice as he stormed toward them, her heart pounding.

To be continued...

CHAPTER 32- TE AMO

Malachi emerged from the hole, looking unimpressed. "You got a problem?" he drawled as if the idea was absurd.

The red in his eyes pulsed. "Yeah," he growled, his voice a low rumble, "you killed my baby cousin. I can't let that slide."

Miguel and Bianca followed Malachi, taking up positions on either side of Malachi.

Miguel said, "You talking about the crazy girl? Yeah, he didn't do that."

The red-eyed man cocked his head, disbelief etched on his face. "Are you kidding me?" he scoffed.

"Okay," he said, pointing at Malachi. "I'm going to kill you." Then, pointing at Bianca, he added, "And you, I'm going to need your powers." Finally, he turned to Miguel. "I'll talk to you later."

Miguel started to protest, The red-eyed man's mouth opened, revealing not a tongue, but a churning inferno of red flames. With a guttural roar, he expelled a jet of fire, a blazing projectile that shot toward Malachi like a rocket.

The crimson arrow was almost upon him when Malachi's palm erupted in white light. A wave of pure energy, impossibly fast, slammed into the oncoming fire, the collision creating a blinding explosion.

The impact was devastating. The blast obliterated the walls, floor, and ceiling, leaving only a gaping chasm. Bianca's jaw dropped in shock. Silence reigned for a moment, broken only by the hiss of escaping steam. Then, Malachi looked at his hand, a tremor running through him. He slowly clenched his fist, his gaze piercing the smoke, a storm brewing within his eye.

Malachi seized his chance and lunged at the man. Miguel yelled, "Bro!"

Malachi moved with blinding speed, his punch aimed with deadly precision. The red-eyed man blocked with his forearm, a grunt of pain escaping him.

Malachi went for a sweeping kick, but the red-eyed man reacted faster than expected.

With a sudden burst, he propelled himself over Malachi, completely catching him off guard. Before he could react, a blue fire fist slammed into the man's face from behind, sending him crashing into the wall of the sterile corridor.

The corridor was stark, with fluorescent lights casting a harsh glow on the polished floors. Doors lined both sides, their surfaces reflecting the light.

The red-eyed man rebounded from the wall, a dazed look in his eyes. Blood streamed from a split lip as he coughed, spitting out a mixture of blood and broken teeth.

Miguel stood next to Malachi, his gaze fixed on the injured man, the tension in the air palpable as they prepared for the next move.

Miguel retorted, "What's wrong with me? What's wrong with you?"

A quick tap on his shoulder. He turned with a low "mh," but it was too late. Bianca's jab was a blur of motion, precise and deadly.

The twins reacted instantly, stepping aside as he rocketed between them, a human missile.

Bianca walked toward the embedded figure, her face a mask of cold fury. She leaned in, her voice low and dangerous.

"That's for lying to me, doofus," she hissed, the words laced with contempt. Straightening up, she addressed the twins. "Can we go now?"

"Yes, ma'am," Miguel replied with a grin.

Malachi saw him— the red-eyed figure behind Bianca. With startling speed, the man seized Bianca's neck, hurling her down the left hallway. Her wings wrapped around her protectively as she smashed through the twin doors, leaving a swirl of feathers and a hint of blood.

The stranger, blood on his chin, mocked, "Girls, always in such a rush." Enraged, Malachi charged, but his limbs were encased in molten rock. Bianca struggled nearby, similarly trapped.

He swaggered toward Malachi, a smirk playing on his lips. "Last time? You won, yes. But let's be clear: I was holding back. Necessary reasons, naturally," he said, his voice dripping with condescension.

Miguel, seeing the danger, focused his energy, his palm glowing intensely blue. "Watch it. You better Let him go," he commanded, his voice steady.

The guy paused, smirking. "So it's like that?"

Miguel stood firm, his expression defiant and loyal. "What do you mean, 'it's like that'? That's my brother," he asserted, his voice rich with conviction.

The guy chuckled, then snapped his head up, his gaze sharp. "Stop calling him that! He's not your brother," he barked.

Miguel stood resolute, his eyes blazing. "We share the same mom and dad. We're brothers, and being twins—that's even deeper," he declared.

The man scrutinized Malachi, asserting with chilling certainty, "Yes, you're indeed a twin, but it's not with him." He gestured towards Malachi with a knowing nod.

"That girl he killed—she was your twin." Miguel glanced at Malachi, a flicker of doubt momentarily crossing his face. Internally, Malachi pleaded, *No, Miguel, don't believe him.*

"Let me tell you a story," the man said, leaning in. He recounted events from the day Miguel was born, pointing at Malachi with each detail. Malachi braced himself for the inevitable lie.

The man's voice dripped with anger and bitterness as he spoke, "Malachi's family slaughtered ours—your parents, our cousins, our grandparents. Only the children escaped because my mother saved us. I risked everything to return for you," he said, pointing at Miguel with fierce defiance.

The man's words hung heavy, painting a picture of betrayal and massacre. Miguel's hand slowly dropped, his body language shifting from defiance to uncertainty.

"Bro, he's lying," Malachi pleaded, his voice strained. "He's making it up!"

"I'm lying?" the man asked, a cruel smile playing on his lips. "Listen to my heart." He paused.

Miguel hesitated, then said, "Nah, you're not lying."

Malachi's eye widened as an ethereal glow enveloped him, lunar energy pouring into him from the walls. His muscles swelled, clothes straining against the forceful transformation.

The room seemed to pulse with the weight of the revelation, the air thick with the unspoken bond of blood and betrayal.

Miguel's heart ached with the newfound knowledge, the truth unraveling the very fabric of his identity.

The man's words echoed in his mind, each syllable a dagger, carving out the innocence of his past and replacing it with a haunting legacy of vengeance and loss.

Radiant moonlight burst from his body, shattering the molten rock prison in a cascade of fragments.

As this power surged, the white of his single eye turned black, his iris glowing an intense blue. In that moment, memories of his twin shattered like glass within his mind, leaving a haunting clarity in their wake.

He grabbed the man's face, rage twisting his features. "You lying—" he roared, unleashing a powerful fist to the man's jaw.

The man's goggles shattered, bones cracked under Malachi's furious assault. He slid down the wall, his mouth open in a silent scream as left and right hooks rained down.

An intense heat engulfed Malachi, as if the sun itself were bearing down on him. He instinctively raised his hand to shield his face, retreating from the scorching assault. Stumbling back, he saw Miguel's fiery blue palm aimed at him, guilt etched deeply into his features.

"What are you doing, man?" Malachi's voice was barely a whisper, choked with disbelief. Nearby, Bianca struggled within her cocoon.

Miguel's voice trembled. "He said we're not family, that we should be enemies.

But... I care about you. I could never truly hate you."

Malachi's heart sank as he stepped back. "And you believe him?"
Miguel, his gaze unwavering, said, "Yes, I do. He wasn't lying."

Malachi shook his head, his heart shattering. A banging came from Bianca's cocoon. Memories flooded back—the ambulance, the promise to always stick by Miguel, childhood games, hospital visits—all shattering like glass. He felt the weight of the lies, the betrayal.

"Oh, by the way," the man said, "I'm Ronaldinho, but call me Ronnie."

Miguel managed a weak, "Nice to meet you."

"How about we get out of here?" Ronnie proposed, his voice laced with urgency. He paused, then added with a dark edge, "But not before I deal with Malachi," gesturing menacingly in Malachi's direction.

Miguel gently lowered Ronnie's hand, his voice calm yet firm. "No, let it go. Despite everything, I still care about him."

Ronnie shrugged. "Screw it." He slung an arm around Miguel's shoulder and walked towards the door, promising to tell Miguel everything about their family, revealing his true name: Jericho.

They vanished, leaving Malachi slumped against the wall. A guttural scream tore from his throat, reverberating off the walls. Above the chaos, a voice called out his name.

Malachi turned to see Jermaine emerging from the surgery room, shirtless and bloody, his eye filled with resolve.

"What's going on here?" Jermaine asked. "A whole lot of madness," he said, stepping closer. Malachi brushed a tear from his eye and nodded, "I know."

Jermaine asked about Bianca. A purple blur zipped past them, bursting through the hallway doors.

Dre shouted urgently, "Yo, we gotta go! This place is coming down!" Malachi's eye widened in shock at the sight of Dre's missing arm, his sword hanging loosely in his grip. Dre's gaze shifted to Bianca, trapped in her cocoon, and his expression hardened with determination.

"Not good," he muttered under his breath, feeling the hum of his sword in his hand. With a steadying breath, he raised the blade, murmuring, "Let's hope I don't mess this up."

In one fluid motion, he slashed downward, expertly slicing through the cocoon and freeing Bianca. She gasped for air, collapsing into his arm as he quipped with a grin, "See? I might have a future as a surgeon."

Explosions rocked the building. Dre cleaved his sword, a purple line appearing. "Go through it!" he yelled.

They went through the purple rift, emerging outside a fence. Bianca, her wings dissipating, whimpered. Malachi held her, asking if she was okay. They spotted Noah slumped against the fence, charred and bloody.

Malachi checked his pulse. "He's alive," he whispered. Bianca gasped, "Oh thank God!" The others emerged, static clinging to their clothes.

Malachi whispered, "I couldn't lose you too, man," as the hospital crumbled around them.

Jermaine exclaimed, "Okay, what the heck?!" Bianca thanked them for saving her, recounting her ordeal with Miguel. Jermaine's eyes widened.

Dre glanced at Malachi, who stood up, before pulling him into a one-armed hug. An explosion erupted behind them. As the dust settled, Deon and Catherine emerged, Deon clutching his bloody left arm. Catherine, blood trickling down her forehead, spotted Bianca and embraced her. Deon waved at Bianca, relieved.

He noticed someone was missing. "Where's Miguel?" he asked. Catherine looked at Malachi, who shared the news.

Deon looked dumbfounded and yelled, "Huh?!"

To be continued...

CHAPTER 33- CREE

The city's breath hitched, a tremor felt even within the confines of Dre's car. Rain lashed against the windows, mirroring the storm brewing inside. The rhythmic thump of the engine was a fragile counterpoint to the unspoken anxieties swirling among the passengers.

They passed a police roadblock, the flashing blue and red lights a momentary distraction in the periphery, barely registering amidst the weight of their urgent concerns.

The city's escalating unrest was a backdrop to their private storm, their focus entirely consumed by the unspoken anxieties and impending crisis within the car.

Dre, his jaw tight, navigated the slick streets, his usual easy confidence replaced by a grim determination. In the backseat, Jermaine, Noah, Deon, Malachi, Bianca, and Catherine sat huddled, each a silent island in a sea of shared dread.

Malachi, his eye dark with unshed tears, finally broke the suffocating silence. He didn't announce his intention; he simply began, his voice a low tremor against the rhythm of the wipers. "Miguel... he's with them.

Bianca's hand found his, a silent promise of unwavering support. Jermaine, however, remained silent, his usual easy charm replaced by a deep-seated unease. The lie of omission felt like a betrayal, a heavy burden on his conscience.

Catherine's gaze was sharp, her expression resolute. Dre, catching Malachi's eye in the rearview mirror, offered a brief, almost imperceptible nod —a silent acknowledgment of the shared burden, a promise of unwavering support.

The car pulled up to Malachi's house. The familiar creak of the front door sounded like a gunshot in the oppressive silence.

Inside, Ms. Shaka sat cocooned on the sofa, the flickering light of the television painting her face in shifting shadows.

A half-eaten bowl of chips sat forgotten on the coffee table; the scent of stale potato chips hung heavy in the air, a stark contrast to the emotional turmoil about to erupt. Little Malia slept peacefully beside her, a poignant symbol of innocence amidst the storm.

Malachi's heart ached. He steeled himself, the weight of his confession pressing down on him. As his mother's eyes met his, a flicker of recognition, a hint of apprehension, crossed her face. He knew there was no turning back.

Bianca, ever the diplomat, took the lead. Her voice, though gentle, carried the weight of the unspoken truth. "Miguel... he's not here, Ma'am," she said, her eyes filled with a quiet sorrow. "He made a choice. He's with the syndicate now."

Ms. Shaka's laughter was a brittle, desperate sound, a thin veil over the disbelief that clouded her eyes. "That's not funny," she said, her voice trembling. "I know he's just outside. Stop teasing me."

Malachi stepped forward, his hand resting gently on his mother's shoulder. "Mom," he began, his voice thick with emotion, "it's not a joke. Miguel... he protected the man who took Bianca. He chose their side."

The color drained from his mother's face. The truth, brutal and undeniable, crashed down upon her, leaving her gasping for air. "No," she whispered, clutching at him. "This can't be. "Go find him!" she snapped, anger overriding her grief.

The weight of unspoken truths pressed down upon them. Ms. Shaka's sobs filled the silence, mingling with the rhythmic drip of rain against the windowpane. Bianca's embrace held them steady.

She had always known about Miguel's origins. What truly broke her heart was how Malachi learned the truth and the devastating certainty that Miguel would not be coming home.

As Ms. Shaka recounted her memories of the day Malachi entered her life, her voice a fragile thread against the backdrop of her grief, Bianca's quiet strength was a beacon of hope.

The love she'd felt for Miguel, born from an unexpected adoption, was a testament to the resilience of the human heart, a resilience that would be tested in the coming storm.

Ms. Shaka reached out to Malachi, her hand trembling. "Can you forgive me?" she whispered, tears streaming down her face. "I'm sorry for not telling you."

Malachi squeezed her hand, his voice thick with emotion. "It's okay, Mom. You're not to blame."

The words hung in the air, a fleeting moment of fragile peace that offered a brief refuge from the encroaching darkness. But then, it hit them—a wave of icy dread, a palpable sense of malevolence that seeped into their bones.

Bianca gasped, clutching her chest as her breath caught in her throat.

Ms. Shaka instinctively reached for her, her face paling as recognition of the chilling atmosphere washed over her. Malachi felt it too—a suffocating presence that seemed to emerge from the very shadows surrounding them, wrapping around their hearts like a vise.

The warmth of their reunion was instantly eclipsed by a bone-deep chill that settled heavily in the room.

His phone rang, shattering the fragile stillness. He glanced at his mother, who leaned her head against Bianca's shoulder, a silent gesture of solidarity. With a racing heart, Malachi answered, an unsettling premonition gnawing at him.

Through the phone, Malachi heard Captain Mark's voice, tight with urgency. "Malachi, there's been an attack at the clan meeting. You need to get to the stadium right now."

In the background, the menacing roar of blazing flames underscored the grim reality, painting a nightmarish image of destruction as fire consumed everything in its path.

Malachi's eye met his mother's, the storm within him mirroring the city's chaos. In her gaze, he found a strength that resonated with his own—a resilience they would need to confront the impending turmoil.

As the shadows closed in, he felt a deep determination growing within him, ready to fight the darkness and protect the light that still burned in their hearts.

To be continued....

Made in the USA
Columbia, SC
13 June 2025